I0527154

Thomas Stewart Denison

The Danger Signal

A Drama

Thomas Stewart Denison

The Danger Signal
A Drama

ISBN/EAN: 9783337343309

Printed in Europe, USA, Canada, Australia, Japan

Cover: Foto ©Andreas Hilbeck / pixelio.de

More available books at **www.hansebooks.com**

THE DANGER SIGNAL

A Drama in Two Acts

BY T. S. DENISON,

AUTHOR OF

Odds with the Enemy; Initiating a Granger; Wanted, a Correspondent; A Family Strike; Seth Greenback; Hans Von Smash; Borrowing Trouble; Two Ghosts in White; The Pull-Back; Country Justice; The Assessor; The Sparkling Cup; Laura, the Pauper; Our Country; The School Ma'am; The Kansas Immigrants; The Irish Linen Peddler; Is the Editor In? An Only Daughter; Pets of Society; Too Much of a Good Thing; Hard Cider; Wide Enough for Two, Etc., Etc.

CHICAGO:

T. S. DENISON, PUBLISHER.

Copyright, 1883, by T. S. Denison.

CHARACTERS.

CHAS. NORMAN.
ENFIELD, alias Williamson.
CHESTER NORMAN.
DR. VALERIAN.
PETER BULLOCK.
PAT MALLONEY.

PERSIMMON.
STELLA ENFIELD.
MOTHER FORESIGHT.
MISS ANGLE.
NORAH.

Time of playing, one hour, fifty minutes.

COSTUMES, MODERN.

STAGE DIRECTIONS.—*R* means right (the actor facing the audience); *L*, left; *C*, center, etc. The flat is the movable part which forms the rear of the stage. The window in this play need not be *practicable.*

Note.—Thunder is produced by rattling a large piece of sheet-iron; lightning by blowing finely powdered rosin into a flame, or by means of the preparation for that purpose.

OUTLINE FOR PLAY-BILL.

ACT I.

Stella and Chester Norman. Enfield warns Stella. Wreck of the "Northern Belle." Valerian's ingenious theory discovers Enfield's secret. Enfield's burning desire for revenge. The plot. The storm. The rescue.

ACT II.

Enfield implicable. Peter's ludicrous jealousy. Stella fears insanity of her father. Another attempt on the elder Norman's life. Enfield's terrible remorse. The "boys" take Peter "pickerel sticking." Norman's peril. The danger signal.

SYNOPSIS.

Mr. Norman had in early life succeeded by questionable means in obtaining a colonelcy which Enfield would otherwise have obtained. To make amends Norman afterward has Williamson, alias Enfield, appointed captain of the steamer "Northern Belle," which is wrecked. Norman, who thinks W. wrecked the vessel intentionally, had him arrested, and W. flees from justice. He had at the time of the wreck rescued Stella, who is really Norman's daughter, and left her at an obscure place on the Great Lakes. He afterward takes her with him to Bald Point, where he makes a living by keeping summer boarders, fishing, etc. The wreck of the vessel and loss of many lives, together with his wrongs, gradually prey upon Enfield's mind till Stella fears insanity. Mother Foresight knows his secret. Chester Norman is on the Lake Survey and becomes acquainted with the Enfields. Charles Norman, his foster father, calls to see him and is recognized by Enfield. He and Dr. Valerian, who is a pretty thorough knave, allow Norman to depart in a small boat with a squall coming on. Mother F. gives the alarm and Norman is saved. In the second act Enfield plots to throw Norman over a cliff with the tacit acquiescence of Valerian. Mother F. again frustrates their plan and the whole denouement is precipitated.

Enfield's whole soul is possessed by the desire for revenge. In the scene where he meditates for a brief time the allowing Stella to marry Chester Norman, her own brother, as he supposes him, the opportunity for acting is very fine. His part is strong throughout.

Persimmon and Pat afford unlimited fun. Altogether the characters are very evenly balanced. There is not an unimportant part in the play.

THE DANGER SIGNAL.

Time, the present.   Place, the Great Lakes.

ACT I.

SCENE.—*Pine Island on the "Great Lakes." House of Enfield, a sort of summer-resort. Room plainly but neatly furnished. Chairs, some very plain, some better but worn. Sofa toward R. rear. Table L. by flat with papers and books. Map of Northwest on flat C. May also have some attractive steamboat or railroad advertising cards. May have some rustic work such as ferns in wreaths on walls. The whole must be the plain adornments of a home rather than the public parlor of a hotel. Window with curtains in flat C. Doors R and L.*

Pat. (*Taking up the basket.*) Have ye put in the cowld ham, Norah?

Norah. To be sure au' I have.

Pat. An' the chicken?

Norah. Yes.

Pat. An' the bread an' the butter an' the praties?

Norah. Praties! (*Laughs.*) Did ye iver hear the likes o' praties at a picnic? Pat Malloney, you're exposin' your ignorance, ye are, an' makin' a spectacle of yourself.

Pat. I've seen worse things in the woods than cowld praties after trampin' all day.

Norah. What I'd like to know?

Pat. The absence of them to be sure.

Norah. (*Busy packing the basket.*) Hould your blarney and lind a hand to the packin'. Did ye bring the pop from the cellar?

Pat. Aye, I did. These people who come up here to spind the summer for their health consume a dale o' pop and chicken. There's Mr. Bullock will want a half dozen bottles, and Miss Angle will want a half dozen bottles, and Mr. Chester——

Norah. Stop your slander, Pat. Doesn't Mr. Enfield advertise quiet lodgin's by the lake, game from the forest, and the sparklin' waters of Mac-a-chack spring?

Pat. To be sure he does, but I'm of the notion that if he left out the spring an' advertised a pop-factory it would be more conjanial to the boorders.

Norah. What's the difference, Pat, what the boarders drink as long as they pay well?

Enter Stella, R.

Stella. Norah, is everything packed ready to start?

N. I think it is, Miss Stella. Pat, carry the basket to the cellar to keep cool till we're ready.

S. Pat, can we impose on your kindness to drive the pony and the buck-board up to the picnic grounds?

P. Howly saints! I wouldn't drive that pony past the edge of that cliff for all the picnics between here an' Dublin. But I'll jist put it on me shoulder and carry it up. (*Shoulders basket.*)

S. I'm afraid it's too heavy.

P. Faith, I'm thinkin' that compared with liftin' green logs in the pineries all day, this basket is a mere trifle. (*Going.*) Come on, Norah.

N. Indade an' it's not with the loikes of ye I'll be walkin' to a picnic. (*Exeunt R.*)

S. Father has one of his strange spells to-day. I am almost afraid to leave him alone. I dread something, I know not what. I had a queer dream last night in which a strange man was lying in a pool of blood, and father was fleeing for life as if he were the murderer. (*Shudders.*) It's dreadful. This long-continued anxiety is wearing on my nerves. I know dreams are all nonsense, but I can't help thinking of them. And then Mother Foresight has repeatedly warned me that a great danger hung over me.

Enter Enfield, L.

E. Ah, you are here, Stella! I have been looking for you.

S. What did you want, father?

E. I wish to speak with you, girl. Are you going to that picnic to-day?

S. Yes, father.

E. Is Chester Norman going?

S. I believe he is.

E. He calls here often of late.

S. His duties as engineer on the coast-survey make it necessary for him to visit all the different points on the shore frequently.

E. Do they make it necessary for him to take his meals here when he might as well go to the Pine Island House where he belongs? (*A pause.*) Stella, beware of his attentions. He occupies an important government position. Doubtless he has wealth. He certainly has influential friends. You are a poor country girl. It is base in him to amuse himself at your expense.

S. Base! Father, Mr. Norman is a true gentleman.

E. I suppose he is a gentleman, as such things go now-a-days. But consider the difference between you. Discourage him. (*Tenderly putting his hand on her shoulder.*) Stella, if anything should occur to make you unhappy it would break my heart. You are all I have in this world.

S. (*Taking his hand.*) Dear father, I will always try to be worthy of your love, and will do nothing contrary to your wishes.

E. I can trust you. Go now and get ready for the picnic. (*Exit S. R.*) Life has some blessed compensations after all. That girl's devotion is the only ray of sunshine that penetrates the blackness and despair of my life. Betrayed, ruined, and a fugitive from justice, what am I! Ah, I am still her protector, though she is not my own flesh and blood! There is still some pleasure in life when I can live for her.

Enter Dr. Valerian, L.

Dr. Good morning, Mr. Enfield!

E. (*Starts.*) I thought you had already joined the pleasure party, Valerian.

Dr. No, I'm in no hurry. I kept my room this morning to arrange my memoranda concerning some strange psychological phenomena which have occurred in my experience with some of my patients lately. Psychology is a wonderful study, Enfield.

E. Indeed! What does it treat of?

Dr. Of the mind and its workings, of the soul and its secret motives.

E. (*Drily.*) Rather a deep subject, I should say. Mostly guess-work, isn't it?

Dr. Not at all, sir. It is gradually being reduced to the conditions of an exact science. (*With somewhat of importance.*) I think my own labors have contributed no little toward that end. I have advanced several important theories, some of which have been verified in a startling manner.

E. Indeed! Mention some of them.

Dr. For example, it is well known that the face, the form, the gait, the actions, all indicate character. I go a step further and evolve the doctrine of *consequences*. Every human being is constantly bound by a network of influences which are the direct results of his own past acts. A man can no more escape these consequences than he can—if you will excuse the figure—swallow his own head. (*Walks to R.*) He must be Capt. Williamson of the "Northern Belle."

E. I don't understand you.

Dr. I'll explain further (*aside*), and try my theory (*advancing to E. C.*) Every good deed is photographed, as it were, on the soul, also every base deed. When the good are numerous we overlook the base; when the base predominate we often fail to see the good. But the keen observer may read them *all*. We will suppose that a man has been guilty of some great crime and has repented.

E. (*Pacing the floor uneasily.*) Well, get to the point.

Dr. We will suppose he has repented and is now a good man.

E. Well! (*Looking Dr. in face.*)

Dr. I hold that the inquirer who cares to do so may throw the rays of his dark lantern on that particular picture and bring out all its ghastly ugliness.

E. (*Starting.*) Nonsense!

Dr. No nonsense at all. I will show you how. We will suppose the crime was murder.

E. " Murder will out "

Dr. Just so! We will suppose it is burning a house, for instance.

E. Which I fancy would *not* out.

Dr. Not too fast! We will suppose it was wrecking a vessel (*E. starts*) to plunder it of costly goods, or (*with deliberation*) running it on a dangerous rock to be revenged on the owner, thereby destroying many lives of innocent men, women and children.

E. (*Excitedly.*) My God! do you think anybody is fiend enough for that?

Dr. Oh, I'm only *supposing* a case. We will suppose that the crime was the base betrayal of a friend.

E. (*With suppressed feeling.*) Curse the man who will do that.

Dr. So say I.

E. (*Wishing to change the subject.*) Dr., we are wasting the day here in idle suppositions. It is time you were starting for the picnic grounds and I must be at work.

Dr. True, it is getting on in the day. (*Looks at watch.*) I must be off. (*Exit L.*)

E. (*Pacing floor.*) This Dr. Valerian is a charlatan, but no fool. Can it be possible that he recognizes in me the Captain of the " Northern Belle," that ill-fated steamer which was wrecked with such dreadful horrors? What a fatality has attended my life! Robbed in early manhood of a lucrative position by a smooth-tongued, traitorous friend! Ah, Charles Norman, the sufferings and mistakes of my life shall be requited on you, for your treachery caused them. Not satisfied with blighting my early prospects, you allowed the weighty charge of a dreadful crime to be brought against me. My beautiful, angelic wife, maddened by disgrace, died in a maniac's cell. My poor old mother breathed her last a pauper. (*With strong emotion.*) Oh, what an awful responsibility is laid on the soul of Charles Norman. Curse him! I'll be revenged yet.

Enter Mother F. R.

E. Even the dumb brute will fight for its young or its life.

Mother F. Mr. Enfield, such feelings can only lead to crime, shame and remorse.

E. (*Starting.*) Ah, is it you! I am already a criminal in the eyes of the law.

Mother F. But not in the eyes of God, nor in the eyes of those you know best.

E. Pooh! A clear conscience may satisfy some people, but not *me.* It will not restore lost dear ones, nor place me in the high station I once occupied.

Mother F. But it gives sound slumber.

E. (*Scornfully.*) Much you know about it. as I can testify who have tossed sleeplessly many a night.

Mother F. That is because your heart is not right. Henry Enfield, I believe you to be an innocent and wronged man so far as the past is concerned, but so long as you entertain these wild feelings of revenge you are a criminal at heart. Beware! Conquer them or they will yet bring you to a base end.

E. (*Laughs scornfully.*) Mother Foresight, you claim to read the future in presentiments. If you cannot read the future with more certainty than you can judge the past and present, I have no use for your predictions. Good morning. (*Exit L.*)

Enter Norah R.

Mother F. So I get only hard words for good advice.

Norah. What's the matter, Mrs. Blake?

Mother F. Mr. Enfield treats me as if I were only a strolling Gypsy. I know that dreams and presentiments do foretell the future. Did I not urge the Captain of the "Peninsula" not to sail in that storm? I told him that he never would take his vessel into port, and he never did. Enfield treats me like a common fortune-teller. I have been almost a housekeeper for him for fifteen long years. Many a time I have left my own work at home to run over here and help Stella. Poor thing, she was only a child. And she needs advice yet. There's a great burden on her shoulders.

N. Indade she has a dale 'o work.

Mother F. Work is nothing to trouble. I have always been a sort of mother to Stella, and I shall still be, for the young always need advice. When we are the only families on Bald Point I think we ought to be sociable like.

Enter Pat L.

Pat. Are ye goin' to the picnic, Mother Foresight?

Mother F. Why should an old woman like me be going to a picnic? No, Pat, picnics are for young folks.

Pat. Ould folks might go just to give a little importance to the occasion.

Mother F. No, Pat, I'll leave all that to the fine visitors from the city.

N. Miss Angle and Mr. Bullock and Dr. Valerian.

Mother F. The Doctor! (*With air of mystery.*) Just keep an eye on the Doctor. (*Exit R.*)

Pat. That Docther is as full of thayories as wather is full of moisture.

N. Thayories, what's that, Pat?

Pat. It's a new fashioned disase, Norah. An' if it onct satrikes in nothin' but dynamite will get it out.

N. Och ye think ye can blarney me, talkin' of disases. Just as if ye knew anything at all about disases.

Pat. Say, Norah, I want to move the pravious question.

N. What's that, I'd like to be knowin'? Pat, is it crazy ye are? Has the Docther turned ye into a crank like himself?

Pat. Wouldn't I like to be a crank? Because dy'e see when you wanted the choores done all yez nade do would be to turn the crank.

N. Faith the first turn I'd make would be to turn the crank out o' the house.

Pat. Will ye answer the pravious question?

N. If ye shpake in riddles I'll have nothink to do wid ye.

Pat. I asked if you would go to the picnic with me? Just to see, ye know, if I carried the basket straight.

N. This is a free country, an' how could I help meself if you wanted to walk along the road at the same time?

Pat. (*Edging close to her.*) Suppose I should walk purty close to yer up there by the cliff where the road is a trifle dizzy?

N. I suppose I couldn't help meself. The road is none too wide there.

Pat. An' suppose I had the basket on one arrum, like this, an' the other arrum should shlip round yer waist, like this (*puts arm round her*), just to kape ye from fallin', ye know?

N. (*Demurely.*) It would be dreadful to fall over that cliff, so I suppose I couldn't help it.

Pat. An' suppose I should look into yer eyes like this? (*Suddenly snatches a kiss.*)

N. (*Shoving him headlong.*) What else are ye goin' to suppose?

Pat. (*Straightening.*) Faith I suppose ye will break me neck if you try that again.

Enter Peter Bullock and Miss Angle L.

Peter. Pat, we shall start at once and meet at the crystal spring. I believe you attend to the transportation.

Pat. Yis, sur, I'll take the transportation on me back.

Miss A. (*Affectedly.*) Mr. Bullock, why do you mention details? The servants will attend to all those horrid details.

Pat. The *sarvents*, is it? I thought meself a free man an' a volunteer, but faith I'm only a sarvent it seems after all. (*Aside.*)

She's forgotten the time when she was only a chambermaid in Chicago.

Peter. I was only giving a few general directions, Miss Angle.

Miss A. Mr. Bullock, please desist. You make me nervous.

Peter. (*Alarmed.*) Are you ill. Have a seat, Miss Angle. Let me fan you. (*She is seated.*)

Miss A. Norah, go and get my smelling salts.

N. Yis, ma'am. *Exit N. R.*

Pat. (*Aside.*) Begorrah she's high! orderin' people round like a gang of nagurs.

Miss A. (*Spooney.*) Now, Peter, you know I am not anxious on my account, only on yours. I *so* want you to enjoy yourself to-day, and I know you will be very tired if you see to every thing, Peter.

Pat. Yis he'll *peter* out.

Miss A. Why here is that impertinent Irishman. I thought he had gone.

Peter. You may go, Pat.

Pat. Sor?

Peter. You may go.

Pat. Go where?

Peter. Anywhere so you go.

Pat. Yis, sur. (*Going L.*)

Miss A. Now, Mr. Bullock, you must not carry a single thing. You know it is a whole quarter of a mile to the grounds.

Pat. (*Aside.*) When he was in the ould rag business he could carry a load five miles. (*Exit L.*)

Peter. You mean a quarter of a whole mile, don't you, Sophie?

Miss A. (*Banteringly speaks with a lisp.*) Why, Peter, you naughty fellow! that is unkind. You know we city folks haint used to walking, and there isn't a carriage within one hundred miles of this place, I believe. I should have had one shipped here but they say the roads are very poor in the woods. I wouldn't mind the *expense*, of course.

Peter. The expense of making roads might be considerable!

Miss A. (*With air of affected weariness.*) Yes, I 'spose so.

Peter. It won't hurt me to carry your fan, will it, Sophie?

Miss A. No, I guess not, Peter.

Peter. (*Edging closer to her.*) And you'll lean on my arm just a little passing the cliff. You know the road is really dangerous.

Miss A. Peter, your arguments are *so* convincing. (*Loud cough heard outside. They quickly separate.*)

Miss A. I think that is Dr. Valerian.

Peter. What a coxcomb that fellow is!

Miss A. He is quite a lady-killer.

Peter. He thinks he is. I venture if he found you alone here he would make love to you in two minutes' time.

Miss A. And why shouldn't he?

Peter. Why shouldn't he! (*Aside.*) That's cool. I'll try her.

(*Aloud.*) He's coming in. To prove my assertion I'll just give him a chance.

Miss A. (*Indifferently.*) Just as you choose

Peter. Enough said! (*Exit R.*)

Miss A. Dr. V. may have more money than Mr. Bullock, who knows?

Enter Dr. Valerian L.

Dr. Ah! good morning, Miss Angle.

Miss A. Good morning, Dr. Valerian.

Dr. It is a pleasure to meet you thus. I thought you had already gone up to the grounds. I started once but was delayed by a little business.

Miss A. I was just on the point of starting. But as I shall have to wait awhile I will not detain you. (*Peter slips in unobserved and gets behind curtains or under sofa, as is most convenient.*)

Dr. It is a pleasure to be detained in such company.

Miss A. (*Coquettishly.*) You men are all alike. You pretend to think a great deal of us girls.

Dr. Pretend! It's real, Miss Angle, I assure you. (*Approaches.*) When a man looks into such fine eyes as yours he can't think otherwise.

Miss A. (*Demurely.*) I 'spose not.

Dr. (*Suddenly turning away.*) 'Spose not! Elegant language that. (*To Miss A.*) It would be very agreeable if we could walk up to the grounds together.

Miss A. That would be *quite* so nice.

Peter. (*Getting angry, growls aside.*) Mighty nice.

Dr. Miss Angle, I was very sorry to hear that you blistered your hands yesterday rowing. (*Takes her hand to look at it.*)

Peter. Confound his impudence.

Dr. It's too bad you should suffer so. I have a "healing balm" for the skin. It is my own invention. (*Assumes important professional air.*) It's the result of one of my theories of the transmutation of organic force. By the way, I have a new theory touching the social phases of woman. (*Still holding her hand.*)

Peter. (*Groans.*) So have I.

Miss A. Mr. Valerian, are you aware that you are holding my hand?

Dr. Why, so I am, so I am. (*Does not release it.*) Some people pretend to tell fortunes by reading the lines of the hand. Now I go farther.

Peter. Too far, you villain!

Dr. As I was saying—

Enter Persimmon suddenly L. Miss A. quickly retreats with a little scream.

Per. Beg pardon, Mistah Docter. Didn't know you had a patient. Ax yer pardon, too, Miss Angler.

Dr. Miss Angle, Persimmon.

Per. 'Sdat so? (*Bows.*) All right; nex time I'll git de right angle onto dat name sure. Miss Stella jes tole me to tell you it was time to be gwine, for you see de time are expirin' with considerable alacrity. Dat is if de Doctor thinks you are well enough to go.

Miss A. I feel better now, thank you.

Peter. Good Lord!

Dr. It was only a slight derangement of the cuticle. (*Exeunt L.*)

Per. De cute ickle! What in de world is dat organ fur. Wonder if dat haint some of de runnin' gear of de stummick, or some whah in de innards. Dat Doctor is a smart chap. I heerd him talkin' de order day of de human antimony. I b'leive he can give de name of all de giblets an fixin's in de whole body.

Peter. Deuce take the nigger!

Per. (*Whirls round.*) Did you 'dress me, sah? Why, whah's dat man? (*Looks puzzled.*)

Peter. I shall choke. (*Per Whirls.*)

Per. Dat sounds like de voice of a dead man. Wonder if its de ghost of dat man what was killed on de island in '69?

Peter. A capital idea! I'll try it (*In a deep sepulchral voice, slowly.*) I'm doomed to walk the earth and harrow up the souls of guilty men.

Per. Boss, you don't harrow de soul of me if I knows it. (*Bolts out panic stricken L while Peter hastily exits R.*)

Peter. (*Going.*) Oh, woman! thy name is—condemn it!

Enter Chester meeting Persimmon outside. Brings him in again.

Chester. Persimmon, what are you in such a hurry about?

Per. Well, you see, Mr. Norman, I thought I heerd you callin' me.

Ches. (*Laughs.*) I never knew you to respond with such alacrity before.

Per. I didn't know but you was in—in a state of alacrity, too.

Ches. What's the matter, Persimmon? you look just as you did when the bear chased you up at Gull Point.

Per. In fac', I don't feel very well dis mornin'. I feel a sort of—of—prescription of de bilious canal.

Ches. Oh, I understand! You want a vacation. All right; you go with Pat to-day. There will be a swing to fix and boats to get out.

Per. All right, Mistah Chestah. (*Going L. Aside.*) I wouldn't let him know I was scared for 'leven dollars an' a half. (*Exit L.*)

C. I can see why that nigger played sick to get excused from duty for the day, but hang me if I see why he risked his neck in gettin' out to meet me in such haste.

Enter Stella L.

C. Good morning, Miss Enfield.

S. Good morning, Mr. Norman. I heard you had gone North on business. (*Busies herself arranging papers on table, etc.*)

C. I expected to do so, but have postponed my trip for a few days. I have called to-day to see if I might have the pleasure of joining your party this afternoon.

S. We should be pleased to have you with us.

C. I have an engagement to meet an old friend at the " Pine Island House," which will prevent my arriving early.

S. I will delay dinner till your arrival.

C. Thank you. You are very kind. And may I hope for a sail in one of those little boats all by ourselves ?

S. Perhaps !

C. Stella, my surveying party will move up the lake in a few days.

S. I'm sorry for that.

C. Before I go I have something to tell you. (*Approaches her. They come down C.*)

S. Mr. Norman, what you have to say might better remain unsaid.

C. But I love you truly.

S. Remember I am only a poor orphan, while you have rich friends, and I doubt not are rich yourself.

C. Yes, you are poor, Stella, in the *world's* wealth, but rich in all that constitutes true womanhood. Neither am I very rich. Many years ago my father met a very severe loss in the wreck of his fine propeller steamship, the " Northern Belle." That loss, with other reverses, left him only a moderate fortune.

S. (*Shudders.*) The " Northern Belle," did you say ?

C. Yes; why do you ask ?

S. It was such an awful wreck. I have heard father and Mother Foresight speak of it. It always seemed to depress father even to hear of it.

C. It was dreadful, but let us return to pleasanter subjects. Stella, I love you too well ever to give you up.

Enter Enfield R.

E. Are you stealing interviews with my daughter, Chester Norman ? I took you for a gentleman.

C. (*Proudly.*) So I am, Mr. Enfield. Do you dispute it ?

E. No, Norman. I was hasty. But you know we are plain, poor people, and I would know more of strangers before I admit them as intimate friends of the family.

C. I am ready to give any guarantees of my character which you wish.

E. Some other time then, Norman. Just now I wish to speak a few words with Stella.

C. Then I will bid you both good day. (*Exit L.*)

E. Stella, did Norman say he loved you ?

S. Yes.

E. I'm afraid no good will come of this. Do you love him ?

S. Yes, father.

E. Are you sure of it ?

S. Father, I love him very dearly.

E. Foolish girl! What made you give way to an absurd sentiment like this? Norman is rich and aristocratic; we are poor.

S. He is not so rich as you think him. His father lost most of his fortune when the " Northern Belle " was wrecked.

E. (*Starting violently.*) The "Northern Belle." Stella, there is some—some mistake.

S. Why, how strange you act, father. Are you ill?

E. No; there is nothing the matter with me. (*Musing turns up stage.*) Why did I not think of this before? But there is no resemblance between them.

S. Did you know his father?

E. Yes, I——; that is I saw him once or twice. Stella, did he tell you this?

S. He did, to-day.

E. And he really loves you?

S. I know he truly loves me.

E. (*With wild laugh.*) Then let him love you, the more the better. Let him know the heart's deepest joy. I have no further objections. You shall be married. Ha! ha! ha!

S. (*Alarmed.*) Dear father what is the matter? (*Aside.*) At times I fear for his reason.

E. (*Muttering half aside.*) These Normans are proud and merciless. Let him taste bliss and then walk in the deepest paths of shame and disappointment.

S. Father, what is the matter? Speak to me. Are you sick?

E. (*Still in soliloquy.*) Ah, that will be a sweet revenge! So let it be. (*Stella places her hand on his shoulder. He looks in her face a moment, then suddenly arouses himself.*) What did I say, Stella?

S. I think you are not well, father.

E. (*Relapsing into moody state, paces stage.*) That would be a hideous revenge. But the girl—whom I love as my own — (*fiercely*). She *is* my own. (*Shudders.*) That would be horrible. Stella, what did I say?

S. (*Soothingly.*) Never mind, you will be well in a few minutes; you are only dizzy.

E. Dizzy! I'm not dizzy. My head is as clear as it ever was. Did I give my consent, Stella?

S. Yes.

E. Then I recall it. You can never marry Norman. Think no more of it!

Enter Mother F', unobserved, L.

S. But we love each other.

E. (*With feeling.*) Don't say that. Don't say it. It can never be.

S. Father, you are cruel.

E. (*Tenderly taking her hand.*) Aye, as cruel as the grave I might be, but not to you. I would shed my last drop of blood to shield you from harm.

Moth. F. Stella, leave your father with me. I wish to speak with him. (*Exit S. R.*) Enfield, you are queer again to-day. You should not give way like that before Stella; you frighten her.

E. Mrs. Blake, you know my secret, but you little know, you never can know, the horrible burden of it. To-day I was again reminded of the whole dreadful occurrence. Can you blame me for being queer as you call it?

Moth. F. But you brood over it and give way to feelings of revenge.

E. You are wrong. I have even now throttled the demon of revenge.

Moth. F. Since you are innocent why fret about it? The burden of those souls gone to a watery grave lies not on you, but on the unskillful pilot who ran the vessel on the rocks.

E. I was captain and should have been on deck. Appearances were all against me. Everybody believes me guilty.

Moth. F. You're mistaken. I don't for one.

E. Pooh! Who are you? Only old "Mother Foresight," who has a sort of reputation for "second sight" among the sailors of the lakes.

Moth. F. No matter; I'll make people believe you innocent.

E. Pshaw' What can you do?

Moth. F. I'll put a piece in the papers. Then people will know they've wronged an innocent man.

D. (*Laughs.*) That's very good! Who believes the papers? Besides, what can you say beyond the fact that *you* think I've been ill treated. No, let the matter rest. Keep it out of the papers, and above all don't tell Stella. (*Going L.*)

Moth. F. True, I had forgotten her.

E. Be careful. Guard my secret. (*Exit L.*)

Moth. F. Poor man, he'll go crazy yet I'm afraid.

Re-enter Stella R.

Moth. F. Your father is only a little queer to-day. He's all right now.

S. Mother Foresight, can you tell fortunes?

Moth. F. Stella, do you think I am a strolling gypsy?

S. No, Mother, I did not mean that. I beg pardon if I offended you, but you believe in spirits, do you not?

Moth. F. Indeed I do, child, for I have seen them with my own eyes and felt their wonderful power.

S. Then tell my fortune!

Moth. F. You know not what you speak of. What do the spirits know about your future?

S. I thought they might know.

Moth. F. Nay, the power to foretell the future of a human being, or to predict great events, belongs to a higher power than the spirits of mortals. It belongs to the Great Unknown who made the spirits. His secrets are not to be idly sought by incantations and crossing the hand with a paltry piece of silver. They cannot be bought, but are revealed through dreams and the gift of second sight. You would learn of a lover?

S. Why, Mother!

Moth. F. I can read the thoughts of a young girl. There is one who loves you well, and another whose love—did he really love you—would prove a poison.

S. I do not understand!

Moth. F. The first is Chester Norman, the second is Dr. Valerian. Beware! your path is beset with difficulties.

S. Pooh! Who cares for that quack with his everlasting theories?

Moth. F. He would like to pay you some attentions. Beware of him! He is a base man. (*Exit R.*)

S. Mrs. Blake evidently thinks Dr. Valerian cares something for me. Pshaw! He knows better than to make love to me.

Enter Dr. V. L.

Dr. Ah, good morning, Miss Enfield! How charming you are looking to-day.

S. Do not waste your compliments, Doctor.

Dr. A compliment is never wasted on a good-looking woman.

S. Do you mean they are all such ninnies as to swallow every stale compliment they hear?

Dr. Oh, no, not at all. I meant that beauty is always deserving of compliment.

S. But ill-timed compliment is in very bad taste.

Dr. Very true, Miss Enfield. I beg your pardon if I have offended. But do you not join the pleasure party to-day?

S. Yes, I shall go later.

Dr. Why later? Is it not downright cruel to deprive us of your society?

S. Doubtless you will get along very well with the young ladies from the Island House, and with Miss Angle.

Dr. Pooh! The young ladies of the Island House are very dull and common-place compared with the ladies of Bald Point. As for Miss Angle, I hand her over to the ex-rag-dealer and now man of pleasure, Mr. Bullock.

S. In speaking of the ladies of Bald Point, do you mean Norah, Mother Foresight or myself?

Dr. Mother Foresight, indeed! Why, that old hag——

Enter L., Mother F.

Moth. F. Is here at your service.

Dr. The dev—— Oh, I did not mean to be personal.

Moth. F. Thank you, Doctor, for your compliment. Stella, doubtless you are very busy so I will entertain the Doctor.

Dr. (*Aside.*) Confound her impudence! (*Going aside. L.*)

There's a secret in this house. It may profit me to unearth it.
I'm sure I recognize Enfield.

S. I have some work that demands attention. (*Mother F. and
Stella speak a few words apart R. Exits R.*)

Dr. Now, old woman, what do you want?

Moth. F. Old woman! You're very polite. I want nothing
of you.

Dr. That's a—(*Hesitates.*)

Moth. F. Oh, say it if you choose. You can no more hide
your nature than the hyena can hide his.

Dr. (*Aside.*) I'd like to throttle her. (*Aloud.*) I forgot. I
should have prefaced my question with a piece of money. (*Tries
to put money in her hand.*)

Moth. F. (*Angrily sends money a flying.*) I tell you I'm no
fortune-teller. I make a decent living by my own efforts. I
don't want *your* money.

Dr. (*Trying to conciliate.*) All right! Never mind. My mistake was very natural, you know, Mother Foresight. I've heard
that sometimes your prophecies are very remarkable.

Moth. F. My prophecies! I cannot prophesy. Presentiments come to me. I cannot bring them at my call.

Dr. Oh, indeed! So I see. That is a case that comes within
the province of psychology. I myself have some theories in re-
gard to that matter.

Moth. F. I have heard that you have some wonderful theories.

Dr. Well, yes; that is to say—I think I have. (*Aside.*) I'll
try one. (*To Mother F. in professional tone.*) Mother Foresight,
I believe every act, every emotion, every thought of the human
organization is based on some previous experience. The thirsty
man dreams of water, the murderer of a gibbet, the miser of
money, and so on. You have dreams and presentiments. You
told the Captain of the "Peninsula" not to sail. (*Suddenly.*) Haven't
you been in a shipwreck sometime?

Moth. F. (*Coolly.*) Theories will do when they hit, but sometimes they miss. I never was in a shipwreck. Dr. Valerian, *I*
have a theory. Listen to me. What will be the dreams of this
man. He was young and handsome. He had every advantage
of birth, intellect, education and family influence. He lacked
nothing but principle. His oily tongue won the heart of a beautiful, trusting girl, whose love he soon threw aside as a shattered
toy. (*Dr. uneasy paces floor.*) Not content with neglecting his
wife he wished to be rid of her. (*She faces him, front.*) He
brought a shameful charge against her and drove her from him.
She and her child died in a public hospital.

Dr. (*Aside.*) Curse her theory. (*To Mother F.*) And what
of all this?

Moth. F. What of it? What do you think of such a man?

Dr. (*Going L.*) Oh, a man like that, if there be such a man,
must be a—rather heartless, I should think. (*Exit L.*)

Moth. F. I guess the Doctor will not measure theories with me again. He little thinks that I know his history well. (*Exit R.*)

Enter Pat and Persimmon L.

Per. It's mighty queer dat Mistah Chester don't put his appearance into dat picnic.

Pat. Be aisy about young Norman. He'll take care of himself. Faith, Mr. Simmons—

Per. (*Bows politely.*) *P*ersimmon!

Pat. All right, Mr. *P*er Simmons. What is the *Per* for?

Per. To go wid de simmons. Jes as in Malloney de *Mal* goes wid de loney.

Pat. Bedad, how could ye g:t the *Mal* away from forninst the loney? I'm thinkin' a nagur's name is like a Swede's. It's one thing wid the father and another wid the son, but how the divil they tell which is which is what no Christian can find out.

Per. Dat's mighty easy!

Pat. How?

Per. Case de father is mos ginally older'n de son.

Pat. Faith an' did ye niver hear "It is a wise father that knows his own son"? But we must be stirrin' an' git out the traps. Did ye iver hear of a picnic bein' made when it didn't rain? Persimmon, we must be after hurryin'. We've a dale o' things to git. Ould Bullock wants his oil-skin cap an' his top boots an' his rubber coat an' the big umbarel. Faith they must be gittin' ready for Noah's flood.

Per. An' Miss Angle wants her gossamer, I reckon, n' her umbarel 'n her gum shoes n' her parasol 'n her top boots 'n her bangs 'n—

Pat. Shtop, wait till I think. We must be gittin' off for we have to drive round the road. Mr. Bullock, bad luck to him, wants the big tent, too.

Per. Hadn't we better haul up de house?

Pat. Faith I think so.

Per. An' mebbe he'd like de island.

Pat. Hould yer tongue, won't ye, while I'm thinkin' over the list of things. You go out into the woodshed and git the big tent an' I'll show ye how to tie it up. I'll git the other appurtainances mesilf. (*Exit Per. R. after tent. Pat sits and is jotting down things with a pencil, sticking it int> his mouth every word he writes. Reads:*) "The tint, Mr. Angle's coat, ditto top-boots, ditto oil-skin cap, ditto—

Enter Per. carrying an enormous roll.

Per. Dat tent 's a load fur a mule. Mistah Malloney, *you's* got to carry dat tent.

Pat. Bother to ye, hould yer tongue while I'm thinkin'. Ditto Miss Angle's umbarel, ditto her big fan, ditto her gum boots, ditto—

Per. Say, Paddy, dat's more ditto than I'm gwine to carry.

Pat. If you don't hould yer pate I'll break it. Now you unroll that tent and roll it up tight and tie it while I git the rest of the things. (*Going R.*)

Per.   Say, Paddy!

Pat.   (*Turning back.*) What is it, ye African haythen .

Per.   Don't forgit de ditto.   "

Pat.   (*Aside, going R.*) Faith I'll break that nagur's neck yet before the day is over. (*Exit R.*)

Per.   (*Business of getting the tent into a tight roll.*) Jerusalem, dat's a big tent. (*By squeezing and drawing the ropes he finally gets it into a ludicrous large bundle. The bundle should be padded with old clothes or blankets, and look very large.*) Dat's big enough to start a circus in.

Re-enter Pat with an immense armful of gum boots, overshoes, umbrellas, palm fans and odds and ends.

Pat.   It takes a dale o' conveniences to satisfy the wants of city folk. Here's ould trash enough to run a camp meetin'.

Per.   You forgot somethin', Paddy.

Pat.   What's that, nagur?

Per.   The boot-jack!

Pat.   The boot-jack! Merciful powers! Who wants a boot-jack in the woods?

Per.   How's Mistah Bullock gwine to change boots an' no boot-jack?

Pat.   It's little I cares how. I'll not be makin' a gallery slave of mesilf for no man.

Per.   Don't you mean a gallon slave?

Pat.   Plague take your questions. Shoulder the tint an' we'll be off.

Per.   You carry de tent an' I'll carry de ditto.

Pat.   The tint is much the asiest load.

Per.   I'll give you de easy then. I'll be generous.   •

Pat.   It's only a shtep to the wagon. Pick it up.

Per.   Pick it up youhself. Didn't I tell yer it was a load for a mule.

Pat.   You black imp, its insultin' me ye ar. (*Strikes at Per. and so scatters his own load in wild confusion over the floor.*) Ye villain, ye're not fit to associate wid a gintleman.

Per.   (*Laughs.*) Haint seen one lately, Mr. Malloney.

Pat.   Will ye hilp me showlder this load?

Per.   Of cose I will. (*Pat takes hold of roll as he would shoulder a sack of grain. Per. takes hold of the other end, and by a sudden toss throws it clear over Pat's shoulder.*)

Pat.   Aisy now. What are ye doin'? (*Business of lifting again. This time Per. does not lift much.*) Ye're not liftin' a pound. Now up with it. (*Per. gives the roll a sudden shove and sends Pat sprawling with the bundle on the floor.*)

Per.   Golly, I didn't think I was liftin' so hard.

Pat.   (*Jumping up.*) Ye blackguard, I'll put a shtop to yer tricks. (*Rushes at Per. who makes for the door, but runs against*

Dr. Valerian, who enters L, and nearly upsets him. Dr. sends him sprawling on the floor.)

Dr. What the deuce are you doing, fellow?

Per. We were jes' carryin' de things out to de wagon.

Dr. Well it's time you were at it. You have been half an hour doing what could have been done in five minutes. That tent is needed in case of sudden rain. Come, stir yourselves.

Pat. Yis, sur. (*Shoulders tent and walks out L. Business of Per. picking up and dropping things.)*

Dr. Persimmon, Chester Norman is coming across the bay in a boat, so you'd better be lively.

Per. Dat's so! (*Suddenly gets everything ready and exits L.)*

Dr. The air is very close to-day. I shouldn't wonder if that thunder cloud in the west brought a cyclone.

Enter Chas. Norman L.

N. I beg pardon, sir, for this intrusion, but I see no one else about the premises.

Dr. They have all gone to a picnic except the proprietor.

N. Do you belong here?

Dr. Yes, that is if a boarder of fifteen years' experience can be said to belong anywhere.

N. Exactly so. I am stopping over at the Pine Island House. Came to-day on the U. T. Propeller. Do you know a young man here on the coast-survey by the name of Norman?

Dr. Chester Norman? Oh, yes, know him well; he was here half an hour ago.

N. I wish to see him. He is my son!

Dr. (*Recognizes Norman but conceals surprise.)* Ah, indeed! I'm glad to see you. (*Here is my card.)*

N. (*Reads, "Dr. Valerian, Psychologist, Mesmerist and Mind Reader.")* Glad to know you, Doctor.

Dr. Thank you! (*Aside.)* He's not changed much in twenty years. I'll try my theory. Shall you stay awhile, Mr. Norman?

N. I believe so, Doctor.

Dr. Glad of it. I shall have another intelligent companion at times possibly?

N. The pleasure will be mutual, sir. Have you made a special study of the phenomena of the mind?

Dr. Well, yes. Lately I have been devoting my spare time to one particular line, the interrelation of thoughts and the doctrine of influences and consequences.

N. Ah, I do not quite understand!

Dr. To be explicit, I believe that every act of our ancestors, from the first man down, influences our own acts—that we never can escape the consequences of our own acts, and that a secret influence links the wronger to the wronged in spite of himself.

N. There is reason in it, but isn't the influence so small usually as to be imperceptible?

Dr. I claim not. We will take the example of that parent who, for lack of other work, compelled his boys to wheel a lot of bricks from one side of the yard to the other all day long.

N. A salutary lesson! It would keep them out of mischief.

Dr. But the boys will never forget those dreary hours of labor and the uselessness of the task. *Bricks* are stubborn facts.

N. Exactly, but such lessons are wholesome. I believe in discipline at any price. Human nature needs a hard taskmaster as a rule. Speaking of bricks reminds me of a little incident in my own history.

Dr. (*Turning away—aside.*) I've got him. (*Comes toward N. C.*)

N. When I was a Colonel during the late war, a worthless fellow was brought to me for cheating his messmates at cards. I just ordered him loaded up with eighty pounds of bricks, and had him march up and down the railroad track five hours. There was no more gambling in that mess.

Dr. (*Turning away—aside.*) I remember it, curse him. (*To N.*) What was the effect on the man?

N. Why, my remembrance was that he fainted at the end of four hours and lay in the hospital a week. But he got a lesson he never forgot.

Dr. Doubtless he did. (*Aside.*) Haughty and hard as ever!

Enter Enfield, L.

E. Doctor, I'm afraid we shall have a sudden storm.

Dr. It looks so. (*Turning to N.*) Mr. Norman, allow me to introduce Mr. Enfield, our proprietor. (*E. starts but instantly recovers himself.*)

N. Glad to make your acquaintance, Mr. Enfield. (*Advances as if to shake hands.*)

E. (*Suddenly turns away as if to look out.*) Good day, Mr. Norman. (*Aside.*) The traitor! (*To Dr. and N.*) I fear a heavy rain.

N. Then I think I must go at once. I rowed over in a little skiff that doesn't need much wind to capsize it.

Dr. It is hardly safe to start now. It is three miles to the Island.

N. Oh, I pull a good oar. I can easily make it. I must be back to the Island House to dine with some friends at half-past two.

E. It's hardly safe.

N. I've no fears! I'll take a look at the sky. (*Exit L.*)

E. Charles Norman, by all that's good and bad!

Dr. Then you know him?

E. Know him! He ruined my life. I hate him.

Dr. So do I. He once shamefully humiliated me in the army. The fool will be drowned if he starts in that boat.

Enter Mother F, unobserved L. She crouches in window, behind the curtains.

E. Let him drown. The world is well rid of such men.

Dr. No, Enfield, that would not do. His conduct does not deserve that.

E. (*Fiercely.*) I tell you he does deserve it. He has taken life. My wife died a lunatic, crazed by my disgrace. My old father died a pauper. I am an outcast. Now let him die. Besides, we have warned him. He is in God's hands.

Dr. No, I cannot let him drown, though I'd like to see him well punished. What have you against him?

E. That's my own affair. You gave him fair warning.

Dr. And so did you. (*It grows dark on stage.*)

E. Yes, it is now his own affair.

Dr. But it looks like murder. (*At the word murder there is a brilliant flash of lightning followed by an appalling clap of thunder. Both start.*) Did you hear that?

E. Do you think I have no ears? It is too late now, Valerian. He is already well out on the water. (*Exeunt L.*)

Moth. F. And that's the plot to let the poor gentleman drown like a rat. But I'll save him. Oh, what can I do! The men are all absent but those two fiends. What will not the unholy passion of revenge lead men to! The life-boat! But there's no one to man it!

Re-enter picnickers in disorder, L.

Peter. (*Supporting Miss A.*) Are your nerves much unstrung by the shock?

Miss A. Oh, yes, they are quite unstrung. Support me, Peter. (*They cross and exit R.*)

Per. Dey're 'bout gone, I guess.

Moth. F. Where's Mr. Chester?

Per. He's a comin' a 'scortin Miss Stella.

Moth. F. Get out the life-boat, quick!

Pat. The life-boat, is it? Thin there's sombody drownded!

Moth. F. He's not drowned yet. Don't wait an instant! Hurry!

Enter Chester and Stella, L.

Moth. F. Oh, hurry, Mr. Norman! The gentleman who called to see you is crossing the bay and will be drowned!

Ches. It is my father! My God, he will be lost! Come, boys. (*Exeunt all but Mother F. hastily, L.*)

Moth. F. They'll save him yet.

Enter E. and Doctor, R.

E. What have you been blabbing, old woman?

Moth. F. I've been saving a poor man from death by drowning, and I've been saving you, Henry Enfield, from the crime of murder.

E. (*Hoarsely.*) Have a care! Do you know what you are saying? (*Raises his hand threateningly.*)

Moth. F. For shame, Enfield! Would you strike a woman?

E. (*Groans and falls in chair.*) No! no! My God! my God! What am I coming to?

Moth. F. And as for you, Dr. Valerian, so called, I know you and your career of duplicity. This last deed would imprison you for life.

Dr. What! Do you threaten me? I'll throw your worthless carcass over the rocks into the breakers if you say another word.

E. (*Rising goes between them, C.*) Be still, Valerian. Mrs. Blake, have mercy on me. Never reveal this scene. Think what I have suffered. The demon for the time conquered me. (*Continued thunder and lightning till curtain drops.*)

Dr. Are you fool enough to trust a woman's tongue?

E. Yes, I can trust Mother Foresight. She has ever been true. Will you promise never to reveal this scene?

Moth. F. (*Facing them front, C.*) I promise. Go and sin no more. (*Doctor defiant. E. bows his head in silence.*)

SLOW CURTAIN.

ACT II.

SCENE.—*Same as before. Discovered Doctor Valerian and Enfield.*

Dr. That was a narrow escape for Norman yesterday.

E. The fool! He would have been fixed in five minutes more. His little shell swamped just as the life-boat reached him.

Dr. He has learned a lesson he will not forget soon.

E. I'll teach him another if he stays around Bald Point.

Dr. Enfield, has not this gone far enough? Mrs. Blake already knows our attempt. It is unsafe to make a second. The first could have been attributed to his own foolhardiness. The next would be on our own heads.

E. Are you a miserable slave to be treated like a dog? Did he not impose a shameful and painful punishment on you? Was it a mere joke to carry a heavy load of bricks for hours in the boiling sun till you fainted from exhaustion and lay in the hospital for weeks?

Dr. (*Fiercely.*) Enfield, don't mention bricks to me again.

E. Oh, then, you remember your wrongs? Are you man enough to avenge them?

Dr. Norman is a purse-proud, haughty old aristocrat. Some day I'll cane him soundly in public, but I'll not help to kill him.

E. My wrongs require deeper vengeance. Norman, by treacherously taking advantage of information which I like a fool confided to him, became a colonel by the very means which I relied on to elect me. The regiment which I was instrumental in organizing by a trick became his. He became a general, and by the aid of a speculating friend became rich. I remained at home poor. When the war closed Norman built the fine propeller " Northern Belle." As a sort of recompense he offered me the command. Necessity and the entreaties of my wife prevailed and I assumed command. One night in a heavy gale an incompetent helmsman ran the ship on Knickle Nic Point. In half an hour she was a total wreck, and many lives were lost.

Dr. I know all about it. I was aboard the vessel.

E. (*Starting.*) What!—you aboard the " Northern Belle "?

Dr. Yes, I witnessed all the horrors of that night. I recognized you the first time I saw you.

E. (*Pacing floor.*) Don't speak of it. It will drive me mad. I still can hear the raging of the surf and the cries of the drowning.

Dr. Why should you feel so when it was no fault of yours?

E. I should have put a better man at the wheel and kept the deck myself. Norman believed I did it through revenge, for he well knew my spirit. I was prosecuted, released on bail and fled from justice. My wife went mad. (*Turning fiercely on Doctor.*) Now, do you think I have no cause of revenge on Norman?

Dr. Keep cool, Enfield. You certainly have suffered deep wrongs. But then you have the approval of your conscience while Norman doubtless may not. Now I have a theory that when one man wrongs another——

E. Perdition on your theory.

Dr. Eh?

E. Your theory, like yourself, is a fraud.

Dr. (*With air of offended dignity.*) What do you mean, sir?

E. Don't put on airs with me, Dr. Valerian. From what Mother Foresight said last night I think you are not exactly a lamb.

Dr. Mother Foresight! If she blabs any more I'll throttle her, the old hag!

E. No you won't. The man who strikes her strikes me. Remember that. But we'll drop this subject. I see you are willing to fawn at the feet of Norman.

Dr. I fawn at no man's feet.

E. You are free to go when you please and pocket big fees for medical advice. I only hope it's good advice. I must stay here in poverty, an outcast from society. I'll get even. (*Exit R.*)

Dr. That man is a perfect demon when aroused. I wish he *would* cut old Norman's throat. (*Exit L.*)

Enter R., Peter and Miss A.

Miss A. Peter, what a dreadful storm that was yesterday.

Do you think there will be another to-day? (*Miss A. seated on sofa.*)

P. Really I can't say. If the weather should remain unsettled and dark clouds should come up suddenly as they did yesterday, we probably would ketch a storm, I reckon.

Miss A. (*Affectedly.*) Oh, I'm so 'fraid of a cyclone! Ain't you, Peter?

P. Well, Sophie, I can't say I like to have them fooling round.

Miss A. What *would* we do if a cyclone should come. Really, I think I should lose my senses.

P. It wouldn't make any difference. They would be of no use to you. Sophie, what do you say to a boat ride this afternoon?

Miss A I'm afraid, Peter. Just think of that gentleman's being fished out nearly drownded. I know I should look dreadful limpsy if I should have to be pulled out that way.

P. We could tow you ashore first and then pull you out

Miss A. You horrid thing!

P. I'm sorry the storm drove us home yesterday, we were having such a delightful teet-a-teet.

Miss A. Peter, can you never learn to pronounce correctly? It's tayt-a-teet.

P. No matter! Call it tater-teeter or teeter-tater. That's what it was, anyway. At the house here I seldom can snatch a moment with you alone.

Miss A. (*Languishes.*) Oh, Peter!

P. It's so! It drives me to distraction.

Miss A. Why, Peter!

P. Sophie, won't you name the time when you'll be mine?

Miss A. Now, Peter!

P. My heart is bursting. Relieve my anxiety.

Miss A. You, Peter!

P. Speak, madam, to the voice of love! Speak, oh, speak to this poor heart!

Miss A. Really, Peter!

P. I shall go mad if you don't.

Miss A. Peter, Peter, Peter!

P. (*On his knees.*) Distill one drop of the balm of love into the wound of this poor heart!

Miss A. (*Rather sharply.*) Peter!

P. What, dearest?

Miss A. I'm not a distillery.

P. (*Jumping up.*) Why didn't you say so at first. You're cruel, you're heartless, you're false!

Miss A. Mr. Bullock, Peter——

P. (*Angrily.*) Confound your *Peters!* Here I've been laying my love at your feet, and all you can say is (*imitates her*), "Why, Peter," "Oh, Peter," and "Peter, Peter." I tell you, I won't be *poor Petered*. I'm not poor Peter. I've a bank account of one hundred thousand dollars Isn't that worthy of respect?

Miss A. (*Slightly alarmed.*) Mr. Bullock, you are mistaken. I meant no disrespect; of course I respect you.

P. Is that all?

Miss A. Why, no. Didn't I tell you I loved you? But you are so—so—in such a hurry. Don't press me.

P. That's all nonsense. Somebody else has been pressing you. It's that Valerian. I'll break his head.

Miss A. Why, Peter——

P. Now, don't you say " why, Peter," again.

Miss A. (*Pouting.*) You are unreasonable and jealous, and I don't care whether I marry you or not. (*Rises and comes down C.*)

P. (*Passing to R.*) I know what I'm talking about. Let me put a flea in your ear. The Doctor is sparkin' you and Stella and two or three girls over at the Island House all at once.

Miss A. What do I care for that. He's nice, anyway.

P. I'll break his head.

Enter Doctor, L.

Dr. (*Bows politely to Miss A.*) Good-day, Miss Angle. I hope you are well after your fright of yesterday.

Miss A. Quite as well as could be expected. You know I am naturally very delicate. I think I consist chiefly of nerves —and—and—sensibility.

P. (*Aside.*) Confound his impudence!

Dr. Let me prescribe for you. (*Takes her hand to feel her pulse.*) Your pulse is a little high. I've a theory——

P. Doctor Valerian, are you aware of my presence? May I express the wish that your theories were all in——(*pause*) Jamaica?

Dr. (*Pretending he had not seen P.*) Why, how are you, Bullock? Will you allow me to say that my theories have already traveled much farther than Jamaica?

P. Unfortunately they did not stay there.

Dr. No, they are still traveling. (*Turning to Miss A.*) Miss Angle, I had not completed your diagnosis. (*Attempts to take Miss A.'s hand.*)

P. (*Stepping between them.*) Miss Angle, don't you remember we were going boat riding?

Dr. (*Adroitly separating them.*) Mr. Bullock, this is a professional case. (*Takes her hand again.*)

Miss A. There is no hurry, Mr. Bullock.

P. Yes, there is (*Shoves he 't ward the door—gets between them.*) Professional case be hanged!

Miss A. Peter, do be calm!

Dr. There is a lady present.

Miss A. And a gentleman.

P. Where is he? (*They both laugh heartily.*) I tell you, madam, I ll not be laughed at.

Miss A. Peter, you are unreasonable. The Doctor is present only in a professional capacity.

P. It took him a long time to feel that pulse.

Dr. It's an intricate case. (*Gets between them.*) Miss Angle, I think there is slight tendency in your system toward melancholia. You should seek cheerful society.

Miss A. (*Simpers.*) Why, Doctor, I was a real butterfly at home.

Dr. If it wasn't for the cares of business I should like to be a butterfly, too, and flit from flower to flower in such charming society.

P. I never was in the butterfly business, but I guess I can play it. (*Imitates motion of flying.*) Come, now, let's go for that boat ride. There may be a squall later in the afternoon.

Miss A. Your impatience to go is very absurd.

Dr. Must we lose your charming society here?

P. (*Aside.*) I *will* break his head. (*To Miss A.*) When a thing must be done do it at once. That's my motto. (*Takes her by the arm.*)

Miss A. By-by, Doctor!

Dr. Au revoir!

P. (*Stares at Dr. who turns away R.*) Did he swear at me?

Miss A. Oh, no, Peter; that's only a medical term! (*Exeunt L.*)

Dr. Ha! ha! ha! What a fool he is, and what a coquette she'd like to be. He's as jealous as if she were a princess. She used to be sensible enough when she was a chambermaid in the Garden City. Now, since she has fallen heir to a fortune, she is a fool. Such is the power of money. She's struck with me, and the only question in her mind is whether I've as much money as old Bullock. Ah, the girls always liked me! (*Struts admiringly.*)

Enter Norah R.

Dr. Howd'y do, Norah? I hope you are well.

N. Very well indade, sir; I've no mind to be a doctor's patient.

Dr. Doctors are not what they used to be.

N. More's the pity. Faith, if the breath was clane gone out o' me body I wouldn't consult a travelin' doctor.

Dr. Probably not. Now let me give you a little advice, Norah. You are a good, sensible girl.

N. Sinsible girrel. An' whin did you make that discovery?

Dr. I can read human nature at a glance.

N. An' so can I.

Dr. I like frank, simple, honest people.

N. Indade! The simpler the better, I suppose.

Dr. And above all, give me the true-hearted Irish girl.

N. What are ye wantin' now with your taffy? Is it a thayory you have?

Dr. Never mind the theory. I'll tell you what I want. Does Stella see Chester Norman often?

N. (*Laughs.*) Do you think a fine, womanly, true-hearted Irish girrel would be answerin' such a question off-hand? Doctor, that thayory won't work.

Dr. All right; there are other ways of knowing.

Enter Pat R, as Doctor exits L.

Pat. What did the docther want?

N. Nothing at all.

Pat. Then he's up to some divilment, for that's just the case with a man who wants nothing at all. The doctor is a sly one and,plays havoc with famale hearts.

N. An' do you suppose I care for the doctor?

Pat. Av coorse not when I'm to the fore mesilf.

N. Yersilf! Pat, you've a dale of concate. Do ye 'spose I cares for the likes of ye?

Pat. Norah, ye're jokin'. Don't ye know that we were made for each other? Oh, I wish I could shpake like Mr. Bullock.

N. Ye're silly enough now, Pat.

Pat. He goes off like this: "Light o' me eyes, spirit o' me sowl, and tormint o' me heart, I'm dyin'——

N. (*Laughs heartily.*) Pat, ye'll be the death of me if you kape on.

Pat. (*Aside.*) Faith, I knew that would fetch her. (*Gets close to Norah.*) Ye're my jewel, my pearl, my diamond; my—my—my—(*Norah laughs*)—ye're my tobaccy box

N. (*Gives him a slap.*) I'm nobody's tobaccy box, I'll have ye understand.

Pat. (*Aside.*) Be jabers, I said too much! Norah, I meant ye was a gold tobaccy box with a diamond lid, and hinges of—— what the deuce are the hinges of?

N. Never mind the hinges! I won't be a tobaccy box at all, mind you. Now I must be off to my work in the kitchen. (*Exit.*)

Pat. Bother to the girrels. If ye try to plase them and fail they don't like it, and if ye don't try to plase them and fail they like it still worse.

Enter Persimmon L.

Per. Hello, Pat!

Pat. What do ye want, Persimmon?

Per. Seen anything o' Mistah Chester 'round hyah, to day?

Pat. No, but if he's not been here ye've only to wait awhile to find him. He's purty sweet in his ways with Miss Stella.

Per. Dat's a sweet gal. (*Smacks his lips.*)

Pat. An' what right have ye to be sayin' so?

Per. Say, Paddy, did you know dis was a free country? Now, ef I chooses to 'spress any 'pinion dat 'pinion holds good so long as it don't trample onto de constitution or circumvent de liberties ob de press. Well, when I say dat gal's a uncommon nice gal I mean it, and de feller dat disputes it better stan' from under, dat's all.

Pat. I'll agree with you there, if ye *are* a nagur.

Per. (*Aside.*) Nagur! I golly, dese foreigners are sassy. Say, Mr. Malloney, when I speaks to you I calls you by youah propeh epitaph. When you speaks to me, *Persimmon* is good enough; needn't put on de mistah 'less yer want to.

Pat. The divil ye say! It's manners ye're tachin' me, ye haythen. I've a mind to crack your noggin.

Per. I done got no noggin.

Pat. Did ye iver see the loikes o' the ignorance! What for was yer seekin' Mr. Norman?

Per. He tole me to meet him hyah. He's clean gone.

Pat. Gone where?

Per. Mashed!

Pat. Mashed is it; was there an accident?

Per. No, it was jes' done a little at a time.

Pat. Squeezed to death by degrees. Do ye really mane something has happened Mr. Norman? Did he git between the steamboat an' the dock.

Per. (*Grinning.*) He wasn't hurt much. I guess he liked it.

Pat. By my sowl! Mashed and not hurted, an' liked it, too! Where was he mashed?

Per. (*Laughs.*) With dat gal.

Pat. Faith, that's a nice, comfortable way to be injured. How did it happen?

Per. (*Laughs uproariously.*) Did you eber see de like of de ignorance? (*Laughs.*)

Pat. The blackguard's makin' fun of me I belave. Do ye mean Mister Chester is in love? Then why didn't ye say he was love-struck an' be done with it?

Per. (*Laughs.*) Did you eber see de like of de ignorance?

Pat. Stop your laughin' or I'll shake your tathe out. (*Seizes Persimmon by collar.*)

Enter Stella R.

S. Pat, father wants you down at the barn.

Pat. I'll be there immadiately. (*Exit L.*)

Per. Haven't seen nothin' of Mister Chester dis mornin'?

S. No, I haven't seen him.

Per. If you *should* see him jes' tell him I've done bin hyah. (*Exits L.*)

S. (*Seated by table in attitude of meditation.*) Father is very gloomy this morning, and Mrs. Blake looks very mysterious. I have long thought that there was some secret connected with father's life and that Mother Foresight is aware of it. What can it be? I fear that the mental strain will drive him insane. What would then become of us? Well, we were cast away once and God took care of us. I will trust Him again. Where can Chester be? Why did he not come back yesterday evening to see me as he promised? Can it be that he was only whiling away a passing hour as Dr. Valerian has hinted? Mother Foresight has warned me against the doctor. But then he is gallant to all the ladies. Why should he not be to me? He is certainly accomplished, polite and intelligent. (*Sighs.*) Oh, dear! I wish Chester would come.

Enter Dr. Valerian L.

Dr. Ah! how are you to-day, Miss Enfield?

S. Quite well, thank you, Doctor.

Dr. That was a sudden interruption of your festivities, yesterday.

S. I noticed you did not go at all, Doctor.

Dr. No, I intended going but did not get started till the thunder warned me it was too late.

S. We all missed you.

Dr. Thank you for saying so. I think young Norman will go back to the city with his father.

S. I suppose so.

Dr. He has not called at Bald Point to-day. Well, I suppose the anticipation of meeting old friends in the city causes him to forget friends here.

S. Mr. Norman would not forget his friends so easily.

Dr. Still, a little careless you must admit.

S. He has some good reason, I know. Who knows but he may come yet?

Dr. It's not probable. It is now pretty late to run across, and the "U . T. Propeller " passes the Island at one in the morning.

S. (*Rising turns aside.*) Too late! He'll not come. (*Goes aside as if to look out.*)

Dr. Never mind, Stella, we'll get along without him.

S. Dr. Valerian, you have no right to address me as Stella.

Dr. I beg pardon, Miss Enfield. But Stella is a very pretty name and comes so handy. Then, you know, I've been in the house some weeks and am, as it were, one of the family. Do you forgive me?

S. Yes. (*They meet down front.*)

Dr. Then here's my hand. (*Takes Stella's hand. She wipes a tear from her eye.*) What's this? Weeping? Pshaw! Cheer up; Norman is unworthy of you.

S. (*Starting back suddenly.*) Dr. Valerian, he's the soul of honor.

Dr. But a trifle forgetful of his friends.

S. (*With pride.*) I hope you don't think I was crying for *him.* Oh, Doctor, I'm very miserable here, I've so few friends!

Dr. You deserve a better home. May I offer——

S (*Hastily interrupting.*) I shall never leave father. His health is badly broken.

Dr. He worries too much. You should all leave here. I can get you a situation in the city.

S. What can we do without means? I would be willing to

toil every day harder than I do here if it would place father in comfort.

Dr. I can help you.

S. I cannot accept your help.

Dr. (*Turning away—aside.*) She would make a better man of me. (*To Stella.*) Stella, you had better make a friend of me. Your father is in my power.

S. (*Starting.*) What do you mean?

Dr. He is often moody and violent. I know the cause of it. I can hand him over to justice.

S. (*Pleading.*) Oh, don't say that! Be merciful! Do not betray him! What would you have me do?

Dr. That I will fully explain in due time.

S. I'd die before I'd do anything that would bring sorrow to father.

Dr. He is disgraced already.

S. I don't believe it. (*Bursts into tears and covers her face with her hands.*)

Dr. (*Aside.*) Here's the deuce to pay! (*To Stella.*) Please be calm. I really did not mean to hurt your feelings.

S. Disgrace I cannot bear. (*Sinks sobbing into chair.*)

Dr. There need be no public disgrace. It is a secret yet. So long as you make a friend of *me* all is well.

S. (*Rises, wipes her eyes and faces him steadily, C.*) Dr. Valerian, do you speak the truth?

Dr. (*Quails and turns away L.*) Do you doubt me?

S. (*Meeting him.*) Dr. Valerian, will you meet me like an honest man? (*He faces her.*) Do you speak the truth?

Dr. (*Deliberately.*) I do! (*Turns away—aside.*) But not all of it.

S. Oh, we're lost, lost! What will Chester say?

Dr. (*Aside.*) Curse Chester! (*To Stella.*) Think of what the public will say.

S. (*Pleadingly.*) Oh, Doctor, have pity on my father! Don't betray him, will you?

Dr. No, I will not. That is unless circumstances——

Enter Mother Foresight R.

Dr. (*Aside.*) That old woman again! (*To Mother F.*) If you want to tell my fortune, begin at once. (*Produces coin.*)

Moth. F. I reject your money as I scorn your insinuation.

Dr. What is your business here?

Moth. F. You well know. Shall I tell it all?

Dr. I've no time or inclination to listen to your story. If you wish to repeat the second-hand tale of some idle gossiper do so. (*Aside to Mother F.*) Tell, if you dare, what happened last night. (*Exit L.*)

Moth. F. Stella, beware of that man! He is dangerous. Ask me no questions. Take warning in time. (*Exit R.*)

S. Ask me no questions! I would rather know the worst and end this dreadful suspense. (*Paces stage.*) What shall I do? It will be fatal to displease Dr. Valerian and worse to conciliate him. Oh, that I had been drowned when that ship sank! Life to me is a burden. It will soon be a curse. (*Sinks in chair and weeps.*)

Enter Chester L.

Ches. What is the matter, Stella?

S. Oh, is that you Chester? I'm so glad you've come.

Ches. I was detained. I could not leave without seeing you.

S. Are you ever coming back?

Ches. Why bless you, yes. I'll be back just as soon as some necessary business can be transacted.

S. I hope you will come just as soon as possible.

Ches. That I shall, but what is the cause of your unhappiness?

S. Father is not well, you know. I'm afraid his mind is not sound.

Ches. (*Surprised.*) Why, I never thought of that. It would be terrible if he should become insane here on this lonely point of rocks.

S. It would, but then I might be reconciled if that were all.

Ches. If that were all! Great heavens! what could be worse?

S. There are worse things than disordered intellect.

Ches. Stella, you alarm me. What do you mean?

S. I think there is something on father's mind, and Dr. Valerian——

Ches. (*Quickly.*) Dr. Valerian! Has he been annoying you?

S. No, he has always been very kind.

Ches. If he dares insult you, I'll pitch him over the point into the breakers for the sturgeon to pick his bones. What has he done?

S. Nothing. He promised to assist me if I ever need help.

Ches. I trust you will never need *his* help, Stella. Do not trust him. Let me know everything. Write to me often. Will you do so?

S. I will.

Enter Enfield R.

E. Stella, I have been looking for you. Mr. Norman, will you leave us a moment? I wish to speak with my daughter.

Ches. Certainly, Mr. Enfield. (*Exit C. L.*)

E. Stella, does young Norman leave the Island to-morrow?

S. He does.

E. To be gone permanently?

S. I believe he will be back soon.

E. (*Sternly.*) Why does he come back? Why should the rich flaunt their superiority in the faces of the poor?

S. Father, you do him an injustice.

E. I've seen too much of the evil doings of those who have power. Never trust them.

S. Chester Norman is neither rich nor powerful.

E. You must never see him again.

S. Father, you are cruel. Don't ask that.

E. (*Aside.*) I dare not tell her all. (*To Stella.*) I have the best of reasons. Believe me, it is for your good.

S. Can you tell me the reason, father?

E. (*Uneasily.*) No, no; don't ask me! Go away; leave me a few minutes.

S. (*Alarmed.*) You are ill!

E. Only a little excited at the possibility of losing you. (*Tenderly places his hand on her shoulder.*) It would break my heart to part with you.

S. Father, you are not well.

E. It will soon pass away. Go now; Norah will need orders in the kitchen. (*She hesitates.*) Go. (*Exit Stella R.*) Charles Norman is a hard-hearted man. He would claim his child and take Stella away. It would have been a sweet revenge to let Chester fall irretrievably in love with his own sister! Ha! ha! ha! But I will not be so cruel to her. (*Sits.*)

Enter Stella, Chester and Doctor, R.

S. Father, please let the doctor prescribe for you.

E. Nonsense! I am not sick.

S. Do, just to please me. (*Aside.*) Doctor, can't you quiet his nerves?

Dr. Enfield, you have been exposed much to the hot sun lately. (*Feels his pulse.*) You need rest.

E. (*Quietly to doctor.*) Let's not indulge in any nonsense. I am as well as you are.

Dr. Your nerves are badly shattered.

Ches. Dr. Valerian, I trust you will prescribe for Mr. Enfield. I am sure that he is not well.

E. (*To doctor.*) Valerian, I believe I have full as much *nerve* as you yet.

Dr. (*Starts.*) Oh, of course I admit that, but *nerve* is one thing, *nerves* another.

Ches. Enfield, you must listen to your friends, and take something this time, anyway.

E. Young man, you are as solicitous about my health as if I were your father.

Ches. I never had a father of my own.

E. (*Jumping up.*) What! Aren't you the son of Charles Norman?

Ches. I am only the *adopted* son of Mr. Norman.

E. (*Grasping Chester by the hand.*) Ah, I thought there was no resemblance—(*checks himself*)—I mean I like your appearance. Chester Norman, you are welcome to this house whenever you please to come.

Ches. Thank you, Mr. Enfield. (*They talk aside.*)

Dr. (*Aside.*) Rather a sudden recovery!

S. (*To doctor.*) I can make nothing out of this.

Ches. (*Going R.*) I will see you all again. (*Exit R.*)

Dr. He's all right just now—that is if nothing unexpected should occur.

S. Then there is real danger. What shall I do?

Dr. Nothing!

Enter Charles Norman L.

N. Good evening, Mr. Enfield. How are you to-day? (*Offers his hand.*)

E. (*Gruffly.*) I'm well enough. (*Pretends not to notice Norman's hand and turns away.*)

N. (*Aside.*) Queer old chap! (*To doctor.*) Heavy storm yesterday!

Dr. Very heavy! I think there will be another this evening.

N. Mr. Enfield, has my son Chester been here to-day?

E. He was! (*Suddenly advancing to Norman.*) Norman, you must stay with us to-night. It is not safe to risk another squall.

Dr. (*Aside*) What's up now?

N. I came across expecting to meet Chester and return immediately. I think I'll accept your invitation. I've no mind to risk drowning again.

E. Stella, see that a bed is prepared in the small room for the gentleman.

S. I will attend to it at once. (*Exit R.*)

N. I will stroll up toward where the surveyors are encamped. Possibly I may find Chester there. (*Exit Norman L.*)

Dr. What's your game now?

E. Silence! Will you assist?

Dr. I have no wish to put myself in danger.

E. That's because there's no money in it.

Dr. Have your own opinion. It is a matter of no moment to me.

E. You dare not avenge a dastardly wrong.

Dr. I *dare* to do whatever I choose. If *you* wish to get rid of Norman go ahead.

E. It is too late for me to go back. He has blasted my life. He must die!

Dr. What is your plan?

E. Pitch him over the cliff into the bay. It is only a step from the window of that little bedroom. A little chloroform will keep him quiet. You must furnish that.

Dr. I'll have nothing to do with it.

E. I'll help myself at your medicine case.

Dr. How will you account for such a peculiar case of drowning?

E. Norman always walked in his sleep. It will be easy enough to say he walked over the cliff.

Dr. But if the father stays the son will stay, too. What will you do with him?

E. Send him down to sleep in the little lodge built by that old fellow from the city. It's a cosy place.

Enter Mother F. unobserved R.

Dr. Remember, I have nothing to do with this.

E. Except to keep quiet. (*Exit doctor L.*)

Moth. F. More mischief afoot! (*Exit R.*)

E. I must do it! A horrible impulse drives me on. Norman will discover that Stella is his child and take her away from me. (*Pauses.*) If she should discover my awful crime she would always hate me. Strive as I will, something impels me to crime. I'm in the hands of fate. The public lay a score of lives to my charge. What is one more? (*Pacing floor nervously.*) Oh, I shall go mad! Last night I fancied the northern lights painted the words "Northern Belle" on the sky. In my dreams I see again that dreadful shipwreck and the death struggles. Sometimes, when I gaze fondly on Stella, I think of the awful temptation that assailed me when for a moment I wanted to toss her back in the raging waters because she was his child, after I had risked my life to save her. Revenge is indeed a demon. It will yet drive me mad, and then what will become of her? (*Drops into a chair rear.*)

Enter Miss Angle R.

Miss A. Mr. Enfield! (*Pause.*) Mr. Enfield! Is the man asleep? Mr. Enfield!

E. Oh, it's you, Miss Angle! What did you want?

Miss A. I want to inquire if there will be another storm this evening.

E. How can I tell? I'm no prophet.

Miss A. I thought you had got so used to the lakes and the climate that you could tell when a storm was coming. That one last night was quite dreadful. It was very quite dreadful. Don't you think so, Mr. Enfield?

E. It was pretty bad. But whether it was severe enough to be called "very quite dreadful" or not, I am unable to say.

Miss A. I'm so alarmed. Peter went out fishing three hours ago, and I'm afraid he may get drownded. Oh, if anything should happen Peter! (*Agitation mingled with affection.*)

E. Peter! Who is Peter?

Miss A. Why, Mr. Bullock, to be sure. If the boat should upset with him, I know I should die!

E. You mean he would die.

Miss A. Would he really drown?

E. Unless he's a capital swimmer, the chances would be about ninety-nine to——

Miss A. (*With little scream.*) Please don't say that, Mr. Enfield. You put me all in a fluster. Peter is *not* a good swimmer, I think. How could he be, you know, when he always attended to business so closely?

E. Well, if Peter gets into the bay it will be some trouble to find the body at night, but I'll get the boys out early in the morning. (*Exit R.*)

Miss A. (*Screams and drops in chair.*) I know I'll lose Peter yet.

Enter Chester, Persimmon and Pat L.

Ches. Are you ill, Miss Angle?

Miss A. (*Jumping up.*) Have you seen Peter?

Per. Who?

Miss A. Peter—I mean Mr. Bullock.

Per. Oh, yes, we seed him.

Miss A. Oh, tell me, is he drownded?

Ches. He is alive and sound.

Pat. Wid a powerful appetite.

Miss A. Did he get any fish?

Per. Yes'm 'bout a million bites.

Miss A. What splendid luck! Fish must be very plenty.

Per. Not very! Dey was muskeeter bites.

Miss A. (*Impatiently.*) Oh, pshaw! But he must have caught some fish. Pat, why didn't you wait and help him carry them?

Pat. That was an aisy job. He got only one an' used that all for bait.

Miss A. The idea! Mr. Norman, what luck had you?

N. I wasn't fishing to-day, Miss Angle. I had other duties. (*Exit R.*)

Miss A. Persimmon, where is Peter—I mean Mr. Bullock?

Per. He's out in de porch rastlin' wid a big chunk of b'loney sassige an' a quart o' buttermilk.

Miss A. (*Scornfully.*) Humph! (*Exit R.*)

Per. Say, Pat, let's take Bullock out "pick'rel stickin'" to-night.

Pat. Faith, it's a big job to wade through two or three miles of swamp and brush in the dark.

Per. We'll take a lantern.

Pat. I've an illegant *red* lanthern that Mister Enfield got over at the railroad station. It's a jewel av a lanthern.

Enter Doctor and Peter L.

Dr. Did you catch anything, Bullock?

Peter. Not a thing. I had miserable luck. The fish would swim all round a bait and never touch it.

Per. *Night's* de bes' time fur fishin'.

Dr. But not for all kinds of fish.

Pat. An did ye niver go "pick'rel stickin'"?

Peter. Pickerel sticking! What is that?

Pat. Ye jist spear the fish when they come within rache of ye.

Dr. But how do you get close enough to them in the dark?

Per. Dat's easy 'nough. De man who does de stickin' has a red lantern. He stan's somewhah in an inlet near de big lake. De others dey form a sort of circle roun' in de marsh, an' ev'ry fifteen minutes dey holler. Dat wakes de pick'rel. Dey see de red light an' go fur de spot. Dat man hain't a single thing to do but stick 'em wid de spear.

Dr. Isn't it pretty hard work to stick them all when they are plenty?

Pat. Faith, it makes the sweat come.

Peter. Suppose we try it to-night. Will you go, Doctor?

Dr. I'm not particularly fond of such sports. Still *(with wink to the boys)* I think this would be amusing.

Per. Dey jinerally toss up to see who'll git to hold de lantern an' stick de fish. Case you see dat's de bes' place. Howsever, I'm willin' to gin dat to Mr. Bullock, seein' he'd bad luck dis arternoon.

Pat. I'm willin', too.

Dr. He's entirely welcome to my place.

Peter. Do I have a boat?

Pat. Faith, ye don't. Ye stand in the wather.

Per. De boat would wobble, you know, an' scare de pick'rel. Let's be gittin' ready. *(Exeunt L. all but doctor.)*

Dr. I knew Bullock was a fool in love, but I thought he had sense enough to go a fishing.

Enter Stella and Chester R.

Ches. Ah, Doctor, were you fishing, too, this afternoon?

Dr. *(Going R.)* No, I didn't get time. *(Aside.)* He's got a bite, I guess. *(Exit L.)*

S. I'm so sorry you are going away to-morrow, Chester. *(They come toward front C.)*

Ches. I'll be back as soon as possible.

S. I dread to be alone so much.

Ches. Stella, calm your fears. Your father has seen much trouble, but then his mind is in no real danger.

S. Do you really think so?

Ches. I'm sure of it. There, now, cheer up. Don't be a foolish girl. Can you not confide in me?

S. No, I cannot. There is a trouble which is the burden of my life. I have no right to say this much, but it concerns papa, and lately I fear some one else has some clue to it and will injure dear father.

Ches. Perhaps I could help you.

S. I cannot tell you, for I do not know it all myself. I do wish you were not going away.

Ches. I will not go if there is any immediate danger. Does it concern any one else who is here now?

S. Yes.

Ches. You once spoke of Dr. Valerian. Is he persecuting

you with attentions? If so, I will see that you are not troubled farther.

S. Oh, please do not say anything yet! I do not fear him.

Ches. No, you need not. I believe him a villain at heart, but then his conquests can only be over weak girls who are willing to listen to him. And then your father is always able to protect you. (*Looks at watch.*) Stella, I must speak with Persimmon before I go. I will then come to bid you good-bye. (*Going L., exit S. R.*)

Enter Norman L.

N. Chester, I know pretty well where to find you now.

Ches. This is not a very bad place, father. Decidedly cosy, I think.

N. Cosy it certainly is, Chester, but you are wasting time loitering here. Do you know that I have laid out a career for you?

Ches. I suppose every man lays out a career of some kind

N. But yours is to be no ordinary career. Do not ruin your prospects by falling in love with this girl.

Ches. Stella Enfield is no ordinary girl. She is a true lady.

N. Nonsense! She has no education, no money, no position. I forbid it.

Ches. Father, you are unjust to the girl.

N. Unjust, eh? Oh, that's what young folks always say when they cannot have their own sweet will in love matters! We will end the discussion, if you please, sir. I say I will not have it. Do you understand me?

Ches. I understand perfectly. Father, excuse me; I want to see Persimmon. (*Exit L.*)

N. I'm glad the boy didn't fly into a passion. He shows sense in the matter. The girl is very pretty and uncommonly sensible. I can't help admiring his taste, anyway. (*Looks at watch.*) It is getting well on in the evening. I'll take a look at the weather and retire.

Enter Stella R.

S. Good evening, sir.

N. Good evening, young lady. (*Going L.*) Fine young woman, that! (*Exit L.*)

S. I should like to know what Mr. Norman said to Chester. He is so stern. I am almost afraid of him.

Enter Enfield L.

E (*Eagerly.*) Where is Norman? He is not going to row over to the Pine Island House is he?

S. I don't know. There is no danger, is there?

E. Oh, I guess not! I asked him to stay here to-night.

S. I will tell him it is not best for him to go, if you say so.

E. No, don't tell him that. I've asked him to stay here.

S. Father, you look tired. You should retire for the night.

E. I am all right. I couldn't sleep just now. Go to bed yourself. Good-night!

S. Good-night, father. (*Exit S. R.*)

E. There is no sleep for me this night. Stella thinks I am only a little nervous. If she knew all she would despise me.

Enter Mother F. unobserved R.

E. She fears that I may go mad. That would be horrible

Enter Doctor L.

Dr. Enfield, are you still of the same mind?

E. Yes! Are you going to show the white feather?

Dr. I have no interest in this matter.

E. Dr. Valerian, let me tell you a little story. Once upon a time there was a doctor in the great metropolis of the West who was a sort of mesmerist, psychologist, and what not. Mesmerism didn't pay very well just then, and fast living put him into debt. In his extremity he forged a check on Mr. Norman for a very large sum.

Dr. What's all this to me?

E. Wait and I'll tell you. When I was captain of the "Northern Belle," one day a passenger put a little packet into my hands for safe keeping. He never called for it, and it found its way by some chance into my private papers. It contained private memoranda, some of which explained just how money was to be raised. Let me produce those papers and Dr. Valerian will find himself behind the bars, for your identity is easily established with that of Dr. Fowne.

Dr. Have you told any one?

E. Not a soul! Are you ready now to help me and save yourself?

Dr. Yes, on condition you surrender that packet.

E. You shall have it as soon as the job is done. You must carry out our programme. You stroll past Norman's window in the moonlight smoking. Get him to join you in a cigar. Stroll close as possible to the cliff and I'll join you at the right moment. (*Exit R.*)

Dr. That man *is* a madman! The peculiar glare of his eye and the expression of his face all indicate it. It is dangerous to thwart him. (*Going L.*) I'll put Norman on his guard. (*Exit L.*)

Moth. F. (*Emerges.*) This is fine doings! Murder planned again deliberately and above board. I think Mr. Enfield must be insane, or the evil one has taken possession of him! As for Dr. Valerian—well, well, that individual always had him. I'll spoil their plans. (*Voices heard outside.*) Who is this?

Enter Peter L.

Moth. F. Only the fisherman! Good evening, Mr. Bullock. How are you now?

P. (*Gruffly.*) Frozen to death! Where's Norah? I'd like some hot coffee.

Moth. F. I'll see what can be done for you. (*Exit R.*)

P. What a confounded fool I've been to go out there and stand in the cold water of that inlet till I nearly froze holding a red lantern, waiting for pickerel! The thing looks reasonable enough. Animals are attracted by light; why shouldn't pickerel come up to a light and let a fellow stick them? I guess it's because the pickerel has more sense than I have. I'm as hungry as a wolf!

Enter Chester, Pat and Persimmon.

Ches. Why, Bullock, have you been out taking a walk, too? I met the boys down by the swamp.

Peter. (*Growls.*) The man who goes out here after night is a darn fool.

Per. Mistah Bullock, whah's youah pickerl?

Peter. I didn't get any. I don't believe they come to a lantern, anyway.

Pat. Faith, yez didn't wait long enough. It takes a fish a long time to make up his mind.

Ches. Hark! (*Voices outside low.*) Do you hear that? We have disturbed the house.

Pat. It's the master in one uv his cranky spells talkin' to himself. We must git out o' here or the deuce will be to pay.

Enter Mother F., R.

Moth. F. Silence! Come this way; you'll be wanted. Wait till you see the red lantern give the "danger signal."

Ches. What is it?

Moth. F. Come. You'll know soon enough! (*Exeunt R.*)

Enter Doctor and E., L.

E. (*In low voice.*) Everybody is in bed by this time. In half an hour we'll decoy Norman out. He's a very light sleeper, so it will be easy.

Dr. We'll make short work of him. (*Mother F. softly opens the door L. and listens.*)

E. And then my vengeance shall be complete. Doctor, you must let me have the satisfaction of hurling him over the cliff.

Dr. All right.

E. It is time now. We need wait no longer. Come! (*Mother F. exposes the lantern and flashes a red light into the room crying, "Help, help!"*)

Dr. What does this mean?

E. Discovered!

Dr. Burglars, I should say

Chester, Pat, Persimmon and Bullock rush in L.

Ches. Villains, surrender!

Dr. (*Pulls a pistol.*) Who are you? (*Chester dashes pistol aside and seizes doctor by the throat. Persimmon and Pat seize Enfield.*)

E. Do you assault a man in his own house?

Pat. Faith, it's to keep yez from saltin' somebody else.

Ches. (*As doctor attempts to release himself.*) Keep still awhile, my boy. We want a little explanation of this affair.

Dr. Sir, you have no right to demand explanations. Release me!

Ches. Time enough for that. We find you under suspicious circumstances. Explanations are in order.

E. Do not ask them, Chester.

Ches. Painful as it may be, some clearing up of this affair is necessary It cannot be covered up.

E. (*Bows his head.*) So be it. Mrs. Blake, go on.

Enter Norman, Stella, Norah and Miss A. R. hastily dressed.

N. What is the cause of this disturbance?

Pat. I belave it's larceny or felony or heresy, some such violent crime.

Moth. F. That man (*pointing to doctor*) and Mr. Enfield, who is half crazed, have plotted a crime.

Dr. Who are you, woman? '

Moth. F. Oh, I know you well, Dr. Valerian., When you were only plain Dr. Fowne you married my only sister, a mere child in her innocence and beauty. Your neglect of her and your disgraceful conduct caused her to die of a broken heart.

Dr. (*Sarcastically.*) Is that all? Mr. Norman, release me. I am answerable. (*Chester releases him.*)

N. Mother Foresight, what is the crime you charge against these men?

Moth. F. A plot to murder you, sir.

Miss A. Murder! That's too awful quite! Are you hurt, Peter?

Peter. No, I'm safe, dear.

N. Mr. Enfield, have you nothing to say in your defense.

E. Yes, Norman, I have much to say. I am not Enfield, but Captain Williamson of the " Northern Belle!"

N. (*Starting.*) You Captain Williamson!

E. Norman, I owe all my misery to you. You robbed me of a high position in the army; you disgraced and ruined me as a sailor. I have twice attempted your life. Do with me as you will.

Stella. (*Flinging her arms around him.*) Oh, father, father, we are ruined! (*To N.*) He was not in his right mind!

E. Stella, I am indeed ruined, but there is happiness in store for you. (*To Norman.*) Mr. Norman, you remember that your little daughter, in charge of a nurse, took passage on the " Northern Belle."

N. How can I ever forget it!

E. On that dreadful night the nurse was lost, but I saved the child. I restore her to you now. Stella, here is your father!

N. What, my child! This my child! Can it be true?

E. It is true.

Stella. My father! Is this strange, proud man my father?

Moth. F. He is!

N. My child! My precious child! (*Clasps her in his arms.*)

E. I have nothing left to live for now.

Stella. (*Going to Enfield.*) I will never leave you. You are the only father I ever knew. I can never forget your kindness. Mr. Norman, may I not stay? This poor old man has suffered too much already.

N. Williamson, or Enfield, I have indeed wronged you. I tried to make amends when I placed you as commander of my vessel. That awful disaster ruined all. You may have been careless, but I now believe you were innocent of crime. Will you forgive me?

E. Can you forgive me after what I have attempted?

N. The shattered, broken mind of a man driven to despera-tion is not always responsible. I freely forgive. (*They shake hands.*) Stella will come to live with me, and you must quit this place and live near us.

Stella. That will be so nice, and Chester—oh, I never thought —he is my brother! (*Sadly.*) Mr. Norman, I will stay here.

E. Poor child! I dreaded this. The blow has fallen on you at last instead of on my worthless head.

Stella. You tried hard to prevent our meeting. I see now why. Well, it's all over.

N. No, Stella, it is not all over. Chester, why don't you speak up like a man? Do you want to marry Stella?

Ches. I do.

N. Then you shall. Stella, Chester is the son of a very distant relative of mine, and I adopted him. My own boy died very young.

Ches. (*At Stella's side.*) Then you shall be my wife, and your foster father here shall be one of the family.

Moth. F. And what will you do with this scamp here?

E. He is innocent of evil intention. He tried hard to per-suade me against this rash step. I wish, Doctor, that other mat-ter was as easily disposed.

Dr. Ha! ha! You believe me a forger. Mr. Norman, what became of that fellow, Fowne, who forged your check for $5,000?

N. He was sent to State's prison.

Dr. So you see I am not that Fowne, Enfield. Mother Fore-sight, you evidently believe me capable of any enormity. I have been a very bad husband, and I am ashamed to say a poor cit-izen. I still am a medical humbug like many of the profession, but thank God I am not an out and out villain!

Moth. F. I knew you had the talent for it.

Dr. I had.

Pat. What did yez do with them talents?

Norah. Whist yer blarney!

Pat. Faith, yez niver could find a napkin big enough to hould them.

Per. Mus 'a rented a warehouse to store 'em in.

Pat. Faith I think——

Norah. Pat, let yer betters talk.

Dr. I have been a bad man and deserve the scorn of honest men. I have disgraced my family and brought shame to my friends. It would be useless to say anything in my defense now. But this I will say, I have done much good, too. My life is not all evil. Mrs. Blake, you warned Stella of me, and rightly, too. But as God is my judge I never entertained an evil thought against her. Try to temper your judgment with mercy.

Moth. F. Thank heaven, all is well at last!

Miss A. And Peter, too!

Peter. Nonsense, my dear! *I* can take care of myself, I fancy.

Per. (*Aside.*) An' a pickerl, too.

N. We may all be thankful that things have proved no worse.

E. To you, Mrs. Blake, we owe this fortunate termination of what might have been a sad night for us all.

Pat. (*Taking up lantern.*) An' I'll be afther takin' good care of THE DANGER SIGNAL!

SITUATIONS.

C.

R.
Miss A., Peter, Dr.   Nor., Stel.,Ches., En., Mrs.B.   L.
Pat, Norah, Per

CURTAIN.

NOTHING BETTER than the SCRAP BOOK RECITATION SERIES.

Now Ready, No. 1.

Price, postpaid.   Paper, 25 cents.

"The selections are choice in quality and in large variety."—*Inter-Ocean*, Chicago.

"It excels anything we have seen for the purpose."—*Eclectic Teacher*.

"The latest and best things from our popular writers appear here."—*Normal Teacher*.

CONTENTS OF NO. 1.

Keep the Mill A-going.
Faces in the Fire.
In School Days.
The Two Roads.
Extreme Unction.
Baron Grimalkin's Death.
Words and Their Uses.
Fritz's Troubles.
Two Christmas Eves.
An Interview Between the School Directors and the Janitor.
To the Memory of the late Brigham Young.
How Liab and I Parted.
Old Grimes' Hen.
The Average Modern Traveler.
At My Mother's Grave.
The Newsboy's Debt.
Mrs. Potts' Dissipated Husband.
I See the Point.
The Professor in Shafts.
Mr. Sprechelheimer's Mistake.
God's Time.
The Little Folks.
The Old Schoolmaster.
The Revolutionary Rising.
Pat's Letter.
How to Go to Sleep.
Nothing.
De Pen and De Swoard.
A Greyport Legend—1797.
The Life-Boat is a gallant Bark.
Birthday Gifts.
The Superfluous Man.
Sockery Setting a Hen.
The Water that Has Passed.
Medley—Mary's Little Lamb.
The Launch of the Ship.
Aunt Kindly.
Evening at the Farm.
Battle of Beal An' Duine.
Passing Away.
Mark Twain and the Interviewer.
Daybreak.
True Life.
Modern Loyalty.
Unfinished Still.
Allow for the Crawl.
The Silent Tower of Bottreaux.
Gentility.
The Drunkard.
The Poetical Patch Quilt.
What is Life?
Art Thou Living Yet?
New Year's Chime.
Song of the Chimney.
A Domestic Tempest.
Common Sense.
How Mr. Coffin Spelled it.
The Old Man in the Palace Car.
Ego and Echo.
A Night Picture.
A Penitent.
Rum's Ruin.
The Babies.
What Is It to Me?
Our First Commander.
Horseradish.
The Doom of Claudius and Cynthia.

For sale by all booksellers, or sent postpaid on receipt of price.

NOTHING BETTER
THAN THE SCRAP-BOOK
RECITATION SERIES.

PRICE POST-PAID. **PAPER, 25c.**

"The selections are fresh, pure, and elevating."—*Missouri Teacher.*

CONTENTS OF No. 2.

Albert Drecker, Pathetic	*Thomas J. Hyatt*	5
Better in the Morning, Pathetic	*Rev. Leander S. Coan*	6
Blue Sky Somewhere	*Vera*	9
Wounded, Battle Poem	*J. W. Watson*	12
Papa's Letter, Pathetic		14
Grandfather's Reverie, Pathetic	*Theodore Parker*	16
The Old Village Choir	*Benj. F. Taylor*	18
At the Party	*Elizabeth Stuart Phelps*	19
Romance at Home, Humorous	*Fanny Fern*	21
The Legend of the Organ Builder	*Harper's Magazine*	22
I Vash So Glad I Vash Here, very Humorous		25
Der Dog und der Lobster, Humorous	*Saul Sertrew*	26
What Was His Creed?		28
Dedication of Gettysburg Cemetery	*Abraham Lincoln*	29
Time Turns the Table, Excellent		30
The Man Who Hadn't Any Objection, Humorous		32
The Soldier's Mother, Sentimental		33
"De Pervisions, Josiar." Humorous		34
A Response to Beautiful Snow, Sentimental	*Sallie J. Hancock*	35
The Defence of Lucknow, Heroic	*Tennyson*	36
A Model Discourse, Humorous		41
My Darling's Shoes		43
The Volunteer Soldiers of the Union	*Robert G. Ingersoll*	44
Life, Compilation	*Mrs. H. A. Darning*	46
The Old-Fashioned Mother		47
De 'Sperience ob de Reb'rend Quacko Strong, Humorous		48
A Heart to Let		50
Jimmy Butler and the Owl, Humorous.	*Anonymous*	51
Presentiments, Pathetic	*T. S. Denison*	54
Eloquence or Oratory		56
Raising the Flag at Sumter	*Henry Ward Beecher*	57
Parrhasius and the Captive	*N. P. Willis*	59
Portent	*Celia Thaxter*	.62
He Wasn't Ready, Humorous		63
The Old Clock in the Corner	*Eugene J. Hall*	64
An Illustration, Fine Description	*Rev. Philip Krohn, D. D.*	66
The Seven Stages	*Anonymous*	68
The Bells of Shandon	*Francis Mahony*	69
Circumlocution on The House that Jack Built, Fine		71
The Brakeman goes to Church, Humorous	*Burdette*	73
Address to Class of '77, Knox College	*President Bateman*	75
Bay Billy, Battle Incident	*Frank H. Gassaway*	78
The Flood and the Ark, Humorous Darkey Sermon		83
The Steamboat Race	*Mark Twain*	85
Battle of Gettysburg	*Chas. F. Ward*	90
A Connubial Eclogue, Humorous	*J. G. Saxe*	93
The Chambered Nautilus	*Oliver W. Holmes*	95
Ascent of Fu-si-Yama	*Dora Schoonmaker Soper*	96
The Musician's Tale, Splendid Sea Tale	*Longfellow*	98
Vera Victoria	*H. M. Soper*	104
Ruining the Minister's Parrot, very Funny		106
The Irish Philosopher, Humorous		109

NOTHING BETTER

THAN THE
SCRAP-BOOK
RECITATION SERIES.

PRICE POST-PAID. PAPER COVER, 25c.

"There is such a variety of prose and poetry, pathos, fun and narrative as is not often found in the compass of one small book."—*Practical Teacher.*

CONTENTS OF No. 3.

Flash—The Fireman's Story.................................*Will Carleton*
A Smooth Path...*Millie C. Pomeroy*
The Three Friends, Humorous..................................*Burdette*
Mosses—Earth's Humblest Children...............................*J. Ruskin*
The Nineteenth Century Teacher, Humorous......................
The Blind Man and his Candle, A Fable.........................*J. G. Saxe*
A Thunder Storm, Fine Description.........................*A. P. Miller*
He Wouldn't Hush, Humorous....................................
The Bells...*Edgar A. Poe*
The Blacksmith of Bottle Dell....................*James Maurice Thompson*
What Farmer Green Said..
Napoleon at Rest..*J. Pierpont*
Benedict Arnold's Death-bed.............................*George Lippard*
Soliloquy, Humorous.................................*By a Girl of the Period*
One Cent and Costs, Humorous...........................*Boston Globe*
Poet and Painter.....................................*Miss H. R. Hudson*
Maud Muller's Moving, Humorous................................
What is Ambition? Fine Description.........................*N. P. Willis*
Kentucky Philosophy, Very Funny.....................*Harper's Monthly*
The Problem of Life, Fine............................*Theodore Tilton*
Praise of Little Women, Excellent..................*H. W. Longfellow*
Address to Class of '77 National School of Oratory.......*Pres. Shoemaker*
Rizpah, Fine Pathos..................................*Mrs. Lucy Blinn*
Last Charge of Ney..................................*J. T. Headley*
Decoration Day Speech, Fine Oration.............*Col. R. G. Ingersoll*
Soldier' Re-union.................................*Dr. F. S. Bennett*
Music Hath Charms, Humorous...............*Rockland Courier Gazette*
Am Life Wuf de Libin? Comic......................*Detroit Free Press*
The Diamond Wedding..
The Palace, Descriptive...................................*T. S. Denison*
Driving a Cow, Humorous.............................*Burlington Hawkeye*
A Condensed Novel..
God Wills It So. A Plea and Answer, Temperance.................
Mr. Middlerib's Experiment or Movement Cure for Rheu-
matism, Humorous..............................*Burlington Hawkeye*
Medley...*H. M. Soper*
Vat You Please, Humorous.................................*Wm. B. Fowle*
Opportunity for Effort...............................*George R. Russell*
Battle of Cannæ, Fine Description......................*Eben Hale Wells*
Pierre La Forge's Dream.............................*Eva Katherine Mink*
Quousque Tandem O'Catalina? Humorous..............*Rev. A. L. Frisbie*
Deacon Kent in Politics, First Rate.................*Rev. A. L. Frisbie*
Charge of the Lightning Judge........................*Ray Porter, Esq.*
The Wanderer's Bell...............................*Margaret J. Preston*
A Fish Story.......................................*John Brownjohn*
An American Sam Weller, Humorous..............................
Little Graves, Pathetic.........................*Lillie Surbridge Curry*
Magdalen...*Edgar L. Wakeman*
The First Settler's Story, Pathetic.................*Will M. Carleton*

THE PERSECUTED DUTCHMAN.

A farce, by S. Barry; 6 male, 3 female. Time, 50 m. Dutch comedian the leading character, irate parent and his daughter, Irishman, lover, etc. This splendid farce is always a favorite. Its telling and ludicrous situations never fail to bring down the house. Scenes interior in a hotel.

A KISS IN THE DARK.

A farce, by J. B. Buckstone; 3 male, 2 female. Time, 40 m. This play is so simple in construction that it is very easily presented. The ludicrous denouement of the piece brings out everything to the entire satisfaction of all concerned, and much to their amusement. Scenes, interior.

MY TURN NEXT.

A capital farce, by T. J. Williams; 4 male, 3 female. Leading man, Twitters, an apothecary, just married and extremely timid, walking gents, leading lady, Mrs. Twitters, formerly a widow, walking lady and soubrette. Time, 45 m. Illustrates the difficulties an apothecary encountered through marrying in haste. The sufferings of Twitters are excruciatingly funny. Scenes, interior.

THE LIMERICK BOY; Or, Paddy's Mischief.

A farce; 5 male, 2 female. Characters, Irish comedian, eccentric and irascible old man, gardener, etc., nervous widow and her daughter. Scenes, interior and exterior. Time, 45 m. This is one of the most popular farces ever written.

I'M NOT MESILF AT ALL.

A farce, by C. A. Maltby; 3 male, 2 female. Time, 25 m. Characters, Irish comedian, old man, military man, walking lady, chambermaid. Very funny, and easily presented. Scenes, interior.

LOUVA, THE PAUPER.

A drama in five acts; 9 male and 4 female characters. Time, 1 hour 45 m. Contains a good Yankee character and a humorous darkey character, villain, gypsey crone, etc. This is an intensely interesting and pathetic play. It admits of striking scenic effects, and is a *strong* and popular play for amateurs. Scenes exterior and interior.

Act I., Louva's tyrants. Act II., freedom promised and denied. Act III., the trial. Act IV., flight. Act V., pursuit; death in the mountains; retribution.

"Send sample copy of a play that is as good as Louva, the Pauper. That took splendidly here."—*G. J. Railsbach, Minier, Ill., Dramatic Club.*

"Peleg Pucker, the Yankee peddler, is inimitable."—*Practical Teacher, Chicago, Ill.*

A SOLDIER OF FORTUNE.

A comedy-drama in five acts by Warren J. Brier; 8 male, 3 female. Time, 2 hours, 20 m. This fascinating play can not fail to be universally popular. The plot is well laid, and the incidents decidedly dramatic. Its humor is rich and abundant. Fine opportunities for stage setting. Middle aged gentlemen, young gentlemen, villain, Irishman, darkey comedian, juvenile comedian, old maid and young ladies.

"We were well pleased with 'A Soldier of Fortune.' Do not think we have had a better play."—*W. H. Stewart, Sec. Dramatic Club, Le Seuer, Minn.*

"It is *the* play for amateurs."—*H. J. Hale, Grass Lake, Mich.*

UNDER THE LAURELS.

A drama in five acts by T. S. Denison; a stirring play, fully equal to Louva the Pauper. Five male. 4 female. Time, 1 hour, 45 m. Leading lady, villain, comedian, darkey comedian, soubrette. Strong scenic effects. Storm scene. Scenes interior.

Act I. Conspiracy. Act II. The lost inheritance. Act III. The haunted cabin, the storm in the mountains, Cliffville jail, the regulators. Act IV. Despair. Act V. Escape, capture, rescue. All's well.

"We rendered 'Under the Laurels' to a large and critical audience, with telling effect. It is a capital play and we shall try more of your plays."—*Dramatic Club, Danville, Ind.*

THE LITTLE FOLKS

WILL FIND JUST THE THING TO PLEASE THEM IN

"WORK AND PLAY,"

BY MARY J. JACQUES.

This book is *new* and *novel*. Nothing just like it has ever been published. It combines rare *amusement* with profitable *instruction*. It serves a threefold object. *Public Entertainment, Daily Instruction, Home Reading*. It is a book

FOR SCHOOL, CHURCH, or PARLOR ENTERTAINMENTS.

While nearly all the exercises in the book may be used for public entertainments, Part II furnishes a choice variety of exercises in language, numbers, animated nature, motion songs, and marching exercises, adapted to popular tunes, etc.,

FOR DAILY USE IN THE SCHOOL ROOM.

These exercises are presented in such a pleasing manner that they can not fail to be popular.

They will greatly assist the hard-worked teacher of smaller children in city or country.

"WORK AND PLAY" WILL FURNISH YOU:

Marching Exercises, adapted to popular tunes,
Motion Songs, adapted to popular tunes,
Games in Grammar,
Games in Geography,
Games in Arithmetic,
Exercises on Trees, Plants, Flowers,
Exercises on Animals,
Exercises in Anatomy and Physiology.
The Seasons, Sun, Earth, Winds, Zones.
The Senses, Races of Men,
Industries, etc.

"WORK AND PLAY" WILL FURNISH YOU THE VERY BEST, MOST ORIGINAL, AND MOST ATTRACTIVE

Fairy Plays, Charades, Tableaux, Dialogues, Pantomimes, Allegories, Pantomime Tableaux, Declamations, etc.

This book is original throughout. It displays talent of the highest order. Many of the poems deserve to be committed to memory, and their lessons treasured for life. Everything in it *has a point.*

IT IS A BOOK FOR HOME READING,

Or a choice gift book of permanent value for your little friends.

HANDSOMELY PRINTED, ILLUSTRATED COVER.

Bound in Strong Manila Boards, (137 pp.)..........post paid, 50 Cents.

"Designed as a help in teaching and amusing young children, and admirably adapted to the purpose."—*Boston Commonwealth.*

"Her suggestions are useful, her whole book is very bright, and the exercises suggested are both easily done and effective."—*Iowa Normal Monthly.*

"We can assure our readers that if they want something new and attractive in this line they can find it in 'Work and Play.'"—*Illinois School Journal.*

Amateurs' Supplies.

TABLEAU LIGHTS.

We invite the attention of the public to the merits of these lights. They are indispensable to the proper production of tableaux. In fact a tableau has usually little effect unless strongly illuminated. These lights are made of all colors, but *red, green* and *white* answer nearly all purposes, and are the most popular.

These lights are perfectly safe and easily used. They need only to be placed in a dish or on a brick and ignited with a match.

These lights are put up neatly in packages, each sufficient for two representations of a tableau. Price by express, **50 cents.**

N. B. Please notice that they *can not be mailed.*

Half pound, *by express,* $1 25. Will make eight tableaux. Pound, by express, $2.25.

N. B. In sending fire in bulk we will not send less than half pound of the *same color.*

MAGNESIUM LIGHT.

This consists of a small piece of magnesium ribbon, a metal which may be ignited with a common match. It gives a very brilliant whitish light. Every one should see this beautiful light.

Price, by mail postpaid, twenty-five cents.

BURNT CORK.

Per box, *by express,*.. 40 cents

WHISKERS AND MUSTACHES.

Side whiskers and mustache...$1.50
Side whiskers without mustache.. 1.00
Full beard 1.75
Mustaches and chin beard.. 2.00
Imperial (with wax)... .30
Mustaches (with wax)... .40

WIGS.

At $4.50.	At $1.75.
White, old man,	Negro, old man,
Continental,	Negro, end man,
Iron gray, old man,	Negro wench,
Yankee,	Clown,
Irish,	Chinaman [pigtail.]
Crop (all colors).	

Rent of any wig one night $1.00, second night half price. The person renting must pay charges both ways in advance.

All the above goods are guaranteed to be good.

Wigs, whiskers and mustaches will be sent by mail when cash accompanies the order.

C. O. D.—Persons ordering goods C. O. D. must remit charges both ways in advance. Rented goods will always be sent C. O. D.

We can furnish any article needed by amateurs, whether it is found on this list or not.

www.ingramcontent.com/pod-product-compliance
Lightning Source LLC
Chambersburg PA
CBHW030906260626
47169CB00008B/2719